V. ELIAS

So this is love!

First published by V. Elias 2026

First edition

ISBN: 979-8-9947331-1-0

This book was professionally typeset on Reedsy. Find out more at reedsy.com

Who says that love at first sight ain't real? You don't know it until you experience it!

Contents

Acknowledgments

The book began due to my love for reading books, reviewing books from romance, dark romance and any other genre that would catch my interest.

I wrote this book wanting to share the story of Lucia. A girl that has some childhood trauma due to not having a father figure in her life. She had many obstacles along her journey from childhood to adulthood.

To my husband: thank you for supporting me all the way from the starting point where I told you I wanted to write a book and to the end where I wrapped up the last bit of the book. He was so confident that my book would be an accomplishment and he was so proud of me for going after what I love. He saw me so many times doubting myself because I would tell him that my story sucked and he would motivate me to keep writing. He told me that my story was good. To be honest, some parts of the story were from my own experience and then there are some that are fiction. Even though he knew that some of this story was a part of me, my husband never doubted that this story was very touching and fascinating.

To my son: I want to thank him because knowing that I

was writing a book, I would become busy and my undivided attention would be all in this story. He knew that daddy would be there for him at times where mommy was busy. He was very patient.

To my family: Especially my older sister because she always believes in me. She never once made me feel as if it was not a good idea to write a book instead she always pushed me to write it. She helped me by reading the story and giving me constructive feedback with no judgment.

To my readers: Thank you for taking the time to read this book that I have created. I hope you enjoy this romance book, which also includes some difficult events along the way. From losing virginity to cheating, to making mistakes after mistakes and learning from it to finally finding love. This short story known as a novella was heartbreaking to write but also gratifying because I was able to share a life story that may or may not be related to yours but there will be readers that will connect, correlate with this story even if it's not something they went through or something they did go through.

To all the people that had a rough childhood with no father figure in their life. Just know that you decide your own path on how everything comes out in the end. Lucia's father was a very toxic man, disrespectful, manipulative and narcissistic. I say "was" because it took her too many therapy sessions to build up her walls and boundaries to block him out of her life. Every call and conversation would end up in a fight. Every disappointment had her taking a step back. Every let down made Lucia vulnerable because she could not put through in her head how a father that is supposed to care, love, provide and protect could just give his worst versions to his own flesh and blood. You are the one that gets to make a choice, either you continue letting that toxic person in or you protect your own self and kick them to a curve. Lucia decided on the second option even though it hurt her because she always hoped he would change but no one can't change a person that doesn't want to change. She was finally able to understand that self-love and saving her own mental health was more important than trying to understand his motives or his actions. Please continue to share your story with people, don't doubt yourself and don't make yourself invisible. If you want to write a book, do it! there's no right time just do it! Thank you.

Content Warnings:

- Adult/Mature Content
- Some Sexual Content
- Peer Pressure
- Cheating
- Mental Health
- Eating Disorder
- Childbirth
- Major Surgery
- Infertility
- Emotional neglect
- Long-term Inter-generational Impact of a missing paternal figure
- Father Wound

Prologue

Who knew that love at first sight could be real, I didn't believe in it until it happened to me. Everything in life happens for a reason. I have come a long way from having an absent paternal figure, language barrier, teen peer pressure and everything difficult that comes with growing into an adult. There are so many things I regret. I wish sometimes I could go back in time to do things differently. Mistakes are a learning experience, "We are humans" we are bound to make mistakes and sometimes we make them again and again. We learn, we grow and we do our best to make sure it doesn't get repeated. It takes years for a person to gain knowledge and improve as a person, that is what's made me who I am today. I can certainly say that love can sometimes cure your pain that was caused throughout someone's life journey. I will always be grateful to God because he gives the toughest battles to its strongest soldiers. I was able to conquer my fears, my guilt and my trauma in the end. This doesn't mean it wasn't painful, I wanted to give up many times but I kept going and I'm still here able to tell you my story.

Do you believe in love at first sight? It's hard to believe me if

I said that it was love at first sight! This was a blind date also which is not a very traditional way to meet a person right? I never thought this would happen in real life, maybe in romance movies or soap operas. I feel fortunate to have found a kind loving man. There are so many words I can use to describe him. He is not the typical man you hear in books, he is not a sports athlete or rich but he is a beautiful man inside and out with a great personality. To me that is more important than anything else in this world. I don't need to compare him with all the romance book boyfriends I have because even though he does not relate to any of them, what he does relate to; is that he would do anything for his woman and that woman is "me". He will literally give his life for me and I've never had someone do that for me, yeah— my mother would give her life for me but that's because she is my mother. He chose me because he loves me for "me". I never had that; this is why a father figure is important, a father is supposed to show their daughters everything they need to look at a man, this is how a daughter sets their standards. Fathers show their love with actions and words. That was non-existing for me because my father was rarely present in my life. I felt as if I was always the second option or never the option. This time I am the first option because this man will always put me first! Above his work, friends and family.

Chapter 1 : The Betrayal

Lucia 10 years ago

It's the start of freshman year in high school, anxiety is taking over me, everything is new, new friends, new teachers, new place. Everything is going to take time to adjust. I hate change. The only good thing about it is that I have some friends coming to this new school with me from my previous school. I have never been popular, in fact I'm the opposite. I am a nerd, introvert, and quiet with new people. It has always been that way though. I always try my best to not stand out. My fear of being made fun of takes over, making me the way I am now. I rather be ignored, that way I don't have to really protect myself from being laughed at by people. Being able to speak two languages was seen as a great skill. Spanish is my first language. When I learned English, It wasn't easy but I learned it quickly as a child. It's true what they say that a child's brain absorbs everything. It became so natural that I didn't even have an accent. Most of the people I came with from my previous school have become either popular or have chosen to have their own little group. I always kept my inner circle small. I have only one best friend and a few girls I talk to. Since we were not popular and everyone had their own group "we made ours". My best friend Tatiana has known me since the 6th grade. Tatiana is the girl I confide in for advice. She and I have always been super close.

"Lucia!" Tatiana screamed, calling me from the tables we usually sit in the cafeteria.

"Lucia over here!" she yells again.

I head over to the table we usually sit during lunch. Tatiana and the other girls are there waiting for me. We make our way to make the line to grab some lunch. As soon as we got back to the table, she started telling me all the gossip she had heard from the other friends she hangs out with in class. She knew I wanted all the details."Just because I'm an introvert doesn't mean I can't like gossip." I might not be popular or have lots of friends but that's because I chose to have a small circle.

Tatiana whispers using her hands to cover her mouth.

"There's this guy that hangs out in the field at lunch time that keeps talking about you Lucia." I stare at her with confusion.

"Well, you already know that I'm not looking to date anyone at the moment because of what happened at the end of 8th grade with the boy I was dating for a year."

Tatiana rolls her eyes at me with an attitude, slapping my shoulder.

"Girl stop! That wasn't a relationship, you were a child and that is nothing compared to having a relationship in high school."

"Well Tatiana, I just don't know if I want to go through the heartbreak again. You know that guy I dated wasn't for me, he was hanging out with the wrong people and I had to cut him loose before I was in the wrong place at the wrong time!"

Tatiana groans "Well I think you should just scope it out and see where it takes you. What if you find him attractive and then there is something more there?" I nod, I know she will keep going until she convinces me. I don't want to be the only one with no boyfriend in high school even though Tatiana doesn't have a boyfriend either; She is talking to someone outside of high school which will make me the only one out of the group with no boyfriend.

A few weeks later Tatiana told me that everyone is meeting at the field to eat lunch instead of the cafeteria. I don't mind since it's a nice day out. When I get to the field she is seated with a group of people that tend to hang out here to play soccer while the girls gossip on the bleachers. As I'm walking towards the bleachers, Tatiana gets up to give me a hug whispering in my ear "I'm glad you decided to come to the field because the guy I told you about is out there playing soccer."

"Who is this mystery guy that you keep telling me about? I need you to tell me exactly where he is because I don't know him." She turns me around to the direction of where the guys are and I see a group of boys playing soccer. I find him leaning in to kick the ball to the goalie. He is in his zone, passing the ball to his teammates and looking all good sweating his ass off.

He is tall, sweat dripping down his perfect body, no shirt, wearing shorts that show off his leg muscles. He is showing off his obvious abs, flexing his arm muscles every time he has to throw the ball from the corner field to his teammates.

I'm pretty much drooling just watching him work his magic in the field. As if he knew that someone was gawking at him, he turned his brown eyes my way with a mischievous smirk, he winked at me.

"Tatiana, what's his name?" tapping her elbow to get her attention.

"I don't really know his name." she said.

They all took a break from playing soccer. They trotted towards the bleachers to get their water bottles. I was the closest to his backpack; as he came closer to grab his water bottle he looked me in the eye and then took his chilled gaze back to his friends. Tatiana got up from where she was seated to get close to her guy friend she met in class. She asked him to introduce everyone. Miguel gets near the guy I've been staring at for the past 20 minutes. Speaking loudly he directs his voice to him,

"Hey Juan! Let me introduce you to Tatiana and her friends. This is Tatiana, I have 2 classes with her.

Tatiana bumping my shoulder doesn't acknowledge him or introduces herself, instead she introduces me.

"This is Lucia, my best friend".

Juan looks at me with the smirk raising his hand to say "hi".

I shyly lift my hand to say "hi". Juan goes to sit next to his backpack and knowing I am right next to, he starts chatting with me as if we've been friends forever.

"Are you a freshman?"

"Yeah, how about you?"

"No, I am a sophomore."

We start telling each other the classes we have for the semester and sadly we don't have any classes together. I am guessing the reason for that is because I am a freshman and he is a sophomore.

"You should start hanging with us. I've seen you around a couple of times but never here in the field" He says.

I gave him a slight smile because I know that they usually go out off campus the first 20 minutes and then they come back to play soccer, but sometimes they decide not to come back at all. I hesitate to answer because I don't want to be seen as the boring one. I don't want to mess up getting the attention from him If I decide to say no.

"yeah, I'll see."

I don't want to start hanging with the wrong crowd again or do something that would jeopardize my grades at school. I also don't want to be always "the good girl, the one that never does anything bad" like my mom would always say "I don't have to worry about you because you never give me anything to worry about" which I hate so much because I need her attention on me, not just her attention but to know that she cares about me.

After giving him my short answer Tatiana interrupts

"oh— Trust me we will all be hanging out more, you guys are fun to be around with."

A couple of weeks after we started hanging out with the whole group. I developed a routine where we all met at the field and from there we would either get food in the cafeteria or off campus and then back here for the boys to play soccer. The first time we actually went off campus for lunch, I made sure to be back on time. Juan felt more comfortable around me and now when we see each other during lunch time he goes in for a bear hug. He has become very touchy. He likes to grab me by my waist or shoulders to keep me near him.

"Lucia, you look beautiful today." grinning, he grabs me by the hand. He pulls me to him, giving me a side hug. We pull apart for just a moment then he proceeds to ask me if he can walk me to my class after lunch. I give him a simple nod and he pulls me back in for a hug which feels more intimate. I don't know what he is doing to me, I am starting to feel things for him and I don't want my hopes up just in case. He leads me to the front of the group while the rest walk behind us.

"Lucia, why don't we start walking to your class but let's take the long way, I want to ask you something." Juan says.

I'm nervous, I can hear the beat of my pounding heart. We have never taken a detour before, we have never been on our own without our friends. I give Tatiana a hug and tell her that I will see her after school, she widens her eyes knowing something is about to happen. He starts leading me to the back of the school and away from the group. About five minutes later he makes a stop. I look both sides and there is hardly anyone here. No one uses the back alley to get to class.

"Why– why are we stopping?" with a nervous stutter, he cages me in, I step backwards until my back hits the wall. He gets close to my face for a second. I'm practically shaking. All I can think of is that I really want him to kiss me but I haven't done this in a while.

He caresses my cheek, "Lucia, I noticed the way you look at me and being with you has made me realize that I like spending time with you. I know we've met just a couple of months ago but I just want you to be mine." I struggle to catch my breath.

"I'm starting to catch feelings for you Lucia and I'm pretty sure you are too." "Do– do you want to be my girlfriend?"

My head is spinning, I have mixed emotions and I'm having a difficult time processing what he just asked me. I want to be loved but I'm scared, I need to risk it if I want to be with him. Once I cleared my mind I gave him my answer.

"Yes, I want to be your girlfriend."

Desperate for my lips,he kissed me passionately. We were so happy until everything took a bad turn. We had been going out for a few months and he had already asked me to have sex with him a month into the relationship. He specifically said he wanted me to prove to him that I wanted him just like he wanted me. When I told him that I wasn't ready, I immediately saw the change in him. He was acting as if I didn't want him. I just wanted to wait until I felt ready but he did not want to wait for me. Juan started acting distant, he told his boys that we were being intimate which was a lie but I didn't deny it either when my friends asked me. I didn't want to make him look bad in front of them. A week later Juan came to school wearing a zipped up jacket that was all the way up to his neck. It was odd and suspicious since we were in the middle of spring. It wasn't cold, It was around 70-80 degrees. I was talking to Tatiana by the lockers and her eyes said more than what she wanted to. She eyed me and shook her head as if she was ashamed of whatever she was seeing behind me. I gave her my attention, I put my hands on her shoulders.

"Why are you looking at me like that? What's wrong? Tatiana, what is going on? What is it that you are not telling me?" she sighs,

"Lucia, there's rumors going around that some people saw Juan with another girl over the weekend."

I was feeling hot as if my blood pressure had spiked, I tuned out everything coming out of her mouth because I didn't want to believe it. I wanted to run, she kept grabbing my arm to keep my focus on whatever she was saying. I didn't want to face the reality of the truth but if there were rumors and I was already doubting everything from my experience with him asking me to have sex and him not waiting then it must be true. I need to confront him and ask him face to face, I'll be able to know if he is lying. My heart was breaking into pieces just thinking about it being true. I didn't want to lose him. Why is my life like this?

Why is this happening to me?

"Tatiana, what else are they saying? I need to know all the details. Can you find out?" I desperately needed an answer.

"People are saying that he is wearing that zipped up jacket all the way to his neck because he has a hickey. The girl he was with is younger than you. They are saying that they had sex and that she gave him a hickey on purpose since she knew he had a girlfriend." Tatiana's words punched me right through breaking every little thing I felt for him. She stared at me waiting to see my next move. My feet moved dreading every step closer to him.

"Lucia, wait!— Don't do something you might regret, these are just rumors, we don't know if it's true."

My attention now was being directed at him, he who was just six feet away from me talking to his friends. I stopped right in front of him. Juan smiling went in for a kiss,I swerved to the side letting him know that I was not in the mood for one. No hesitation this time I said, "We need to talk in private" I pulled him away from his friends farther down the hallway where we could talk with no interruption. He grabbed me by the chin "How's my baby doing?" He was too chilled as if he did not care about the rumors that were being said about him. I went straight to the point to ask him about it.

"So— there are rumors going around about you being with a girl over the weekend. Is that true?" He stayed quiet, not even denying it, so I went with the next thing I came here to do which is to try to unzip his jacket to learn the truth. As I put my hands on the zipper Juan stops me aggressively,

"Please don't! You don't want to do this right here, right now!" At this point I raised my voice

"WHY? Why not? It's just so hot in here you must be burning

with this jacket on, you are literally sweating"

Juan stops me again, grabbing my wrists a little too rough. I look into his eyes begging him to tell me what is going on.

"Why don't you want to take the jacket off?Just tell me don't embarrass me anymore. Just– just tell me please." I said. My voice was breaking even before I could finish the sentence. I spoke again with a knot in my throat

"Just tell me the truth"

With a frustrated sigh he knew he couldn't hide it anymore. He let me pull the zipper, and not even half way down, I saw that harsh reality of the truth, it was right in front of my eyes.

A big, red, purple hickey!

No words came out of me, all I did was turn around to leave but then he grabbed me by my elbow to stop me. He starts to zip the jacket back up,

"You can't blame me for this. I asked you to be more intimate with me and you said you wanted to wait but I have needs" I was trying to hold it together without showing any emotion because crying will show him I'm weak. I wasn't even paying attention to him anymore. I kept questioning myself "what did I do? Was it my fault? Am I not enough? Why me?"

Even with all of these questions in my head I know I am to blame because he wanted to be more intimate but since I didn't give it up, he felt the need to get it somewhere else. I pulled my arm from his hold.

"Please don't touch me anymore. This (I gesture with my hand between him and I) It's over!"

A week had passed by, I had put my big girl panties on even though I was breaking apart from being cheated on. After the whole debacle, I decided to isolate myself. I spent time away, didn't have time to hang out with the usual group anymore.

Tatiana was there for me but she also kept hanging out with them. I understood that all she wanted was to fit in. The teen pressure of being popular, fit in; into a certain group and being cool was a priority for most people in high school. Since I wasn't hanging out with them anymore, I barely saw her, but we still messaged here and there. All I wanted was to forget. Juan's friend saw him as the hero not a cheater, but then I was being looked at as the crazy one, the jealous psycho for questioning him. I took time for myself, kept looking forward so I didn't give people something else to talk about. I needed to move on..

Chapter 2 : "V" card

Lucia

Finished freshman year and sophomore year with good grades. At the beginning of Junior year, I was mainly focused on school again and that got me close to a 4.0 GPA. I talk to Tatiana sporadically, and sometimes also talked with the group I used to hang out with, avoiding all contact with Juan. I also hung out with new people I met throughout sophomore year. I started hanging out with a new group, most of them were seniors. I started to notice that I was liking and investing my time with older guys since they seem more mature. They can actually hold a conversation. In art class I met this guy named Luis, who would hang out with all the senior guys. Luis introduced me to the guys he hangs out with during lunch time. I tried to keep my distance about getting involved with any of them. Junior year was the same as freshman and sophomore year, "boring".

Luis usually hangs out with this guy named Eddy, they both

have been very good friends since freshman year. Eddy and I do not share any classes together. Luis asked me to join him for lunch and he introduced me to Eddy that day. Eddy is a year older than me. He has never really shown interest in me and we weren't friends either. We were mostly acquaintances. We would say hi to each other any time we passed by in the hallways or during lunch.

Time flew by, senior year was not very memorable to me. I did start hanging out with Tatiana again since she was no longer spending most of her time with the other group. Something had happened that made her change. I didn't really ask because we both had our own things we needed to work on. I didn't want to be all up in her business and more when we had taken our own routes separately. Tatiana asked me if I was seeing anyone and my response to her was that "I didn't have time for love or little dumb boyfriends." With that she didn't really ask anything else. I had to take senior year seriously as I needed to finish my senior project at the end of the school year to graduate. I was so busy that even when Tatiana would invite me out, I declined. This is one of the things I wished I would have done differently. I wished I would've made the decision to hang out more with my best friend. I wished that all my focus on school would've been less. I just didn't want to disappoint my family or my mother since she had worked hard and had sacrificed a lot of things for me to be here.

At the end of senior year I graduated with the highest grades I've ever had and had an honor roll as well. After graduating high school I was elated to start my new journey. One of them is signing up for the fall semester of college. I took a part time job since I'm an adult with bills to pay. Something that made it easy was that I was still living at home with my mom,

I didn't have to worry about the expenses of rent which was awesome. Everything is so expensive. Working and being a full time student took a toll on me after 4 semesters in. The classes were much more difficult than high school. I don't remember when it was the last time I hung out with any friends. I was becoming more of a loner. I had not made any friends in college either, everyone just goes about their day. They get to class, pay attention and then leave. No interaction unless the professor asks us to work in teams. I had not seen Tatiana since graduation. She went to a different college that was farther away which made our friendship more distant. We still messaged each other here and there but It just felt different, seeing each other in high school was one of the perks we had but now we barely talked. I go to work on the days I'm not in school. Then I go to school full time on Mondays and Tuesdays with a mix of online classes.

One day I got a message on my social media account. The message was odd since we had not spoken to each other since high school.

It was "HIM", Eddy!— he had sent me a private message.

"Hi Lucia, how are you? How has it been? I haven't seen you since high school." I was so baffled I didn't know if I should respond because we weren't really friends like that. What could be the reason for his message?

I decided to still reply and not be rude since I already had opened the message. I was not going to leave him on read— *"Hey I'm good, how are you? I know, it has been super long since we all graduated."*

As soon as the message was sent I saw those little three dots and knew he was about to respond.

"I am good also, I have been working a lot. I just wanted to reach

out to tell you that I loved your recent selfie you posted. You look beautiful."

I blushed like a tomato hoping no one at work would see me like this. I haven't heard anyone call me beautiful in a long time. I did not expect this message to be about my selfie. I decided to be a little bold and respond to him.

"Thank you. You don't look so bad yourself. ♥ *I liked the picture you posted on your account too."*

After I fearlessly messaged Eddy, he sent a heart emoji back. I wasn't really worried after that because to me that was the only message he was going to send "wrong!" He sent another after another and ended up messaging each other throughout the whole week. He asked me for my number so we can message directly without having to go through our social media accounts. We spent weeks messaging and talking about everything. I guess Eddy felt comfortable enough to message me this,

" Hey, I've been thinking lately that we both have been working so much that we deserve a break, don't you think? I'm planning to take a vacation trip soon. I'm going out of town to this recreational park. I was wondering If you want to come with me?"

I was speechless, I didn't know what to answer. I didn't want to say "no" but then all of these questions started to pop up in my mind. "You're still a virgin at 21 years old, you haven't been with someone in a while, do you trust him?" and now this guy that I find attractive wants to take me on a vacation. I didn't know what to do. I took my time responding back. I had to check if I had vacation time at work, needed to ask my professors if I could do extra work to make up for anything that I was going to miss. Let's be real, if I was already asking my job and professors for permission then we know that I was going to accept his invitation either way.

Chapter 2 : "V" card

"Hey, thank you for your invitation. Sorry It took me some time to respond. I needed to make sure I had vacation time, but yes I would like to accompany you on this trip."

"Yes!, let me tell you how much everything will cost. You can send me your half for the park, don't worry about the rest. I got it covered." Eddy responded

I didn't expect him to charge me since he was inviting me. This made me a little puzzled. It was also concerning that he was going to pay for the rest which it had to be for the hotel and maybe gas since he was driving. I put in my head that if he was charging me, that I should look at this as just a friend's trip.

"Yeah, no problem, let me know and I'll send you the money. Also what do you mean you'll pay the rest? do you already have the hotel booked or something?"

" Yeah, I had it booked in advance since I knew I was going to make this trip anyways and there was a discount for it so no worries." Eddy said.

Fast forward to the day of the trip, My mom was so worried that I was going on this trip with him. I never really taken a trip like this on my own and neither with a man. The trip it's about 5 to 6 hours to drive there. Knowing that I was still choosing to go she gave me her blessing and sent me on my way.

Eddy got to my house in his black Camaro, it was a beautiful car. Very shiny, and looked as if it was new. I opened the door giving him the biggest smile I could give and we were on our way. The trip was long. I was silent most of the time due to me being nervous to say the wrong thing or maybe I was just afraid that as long as I didn't open my mouth maybe he wouldn't get bored of me so I stayed quiet. Eddy was chill on the other hand he was just listening to music while he drove the 5 to 6 hours. When we got to the hotel, it was already night time. As soon as we got to the front door of the room, I expected to see 2 beds but instead there was only one king size bed. My inner voice in my head said, "Okay, we are adults, we can sleep in the same bed without nothing happening right?"

That night, Eddy didn't wait for us to get settled in. He got behind me near my ear whispering "I have been waiting for this moment since high school but I never really made a move because I didn't think you would go out with me. I had heard that you were cheated on and that you were trying to avoid boys and focus on school." I was agitated, my adrenaline was going at 100 miles. I did not think anything would happen on the first day. I was already prepping myself that I was going to lose my virginity since the day he asked me to come on this trip but this was way too fast. I hesitated when he got close and personal in my other ear but my inner voice kept saying "When will you have another opportunity to lose your virginity" " You are 21 years old and still a virgin!"

After those thoughts I didn't think twice I just let him touch me. I knew it was for the wrong reasons, I knew I would regret it. I simply wanted to just get it over with.

"Eddy was my first! He took my virginity."

They say that you don't ever forget your first either because you really enjoyed it or because you really hated it. "Well damn right I hated the whole thing!" It wasn't what I expected. It was quick, it wasn't pleasurable and definitely not the right person or the right time!

The next morning I felt so out of place, we still needed to go about our day. We went to the recreational park "I thought maybe this would be the start of something new, maybe my first time was bad but if we keep practicing or he gets to know what I like we can get past the first experience. Right?" Everything was just so awkward between us after what went down yesterday. The whole time at the park he was very distant. I felt strange. I was expecting to see another side of him, maybe more caring. I don't know why the hell I was expecting anything like that, "Definitely not this."

By the time we were done with the park and went back to the hotel, I was quiet, he could sense it which made the room feel tense. He told me that he needed to go buy some stuff and left me alone in the hotel. I couldn't contain myself, I cried so much. I was so stupid, I made a dumb decision, gave up my virginity just because everyone else has lost theirs at a very young age and I was over here holding onto it being 21 years old. Eddy came back later that night and found me already in bed. When he went to lie down next to me the only words that came out of his mouth were "goodnight". The next day, we got ready really early to head back home. The drive was again extremely quiet. As he got closer to dropping me off I became very apprehensive because I knew in my heart that this would probably be our last time seeing each other. I waited for him to say just "anything" but he kept quiet the whole way. When he got to my house I gathered my backpack, went to the passenger side to say thank you for the ride— That's when I heard him say,

"Hey, thank you for being so cool about everything"

"What the actual fuck did he just say!"

"Did I hear him correctly? Did he just say thank you for being cool about everything.."

This only gave away that he in fact used me for sex and I was too stupid to even notice it, I was so determined in losing my virginity and now I am over here with so much guilt. This made me furious at him, at myself for being so stupid. The weeks went by and I was becoming depressed and drained. Isolation was the answer to my problem. I blocked him from my social media accounts and from my text messages. All I wanted to do was forget that I even went with him on this trip. I knew this could've happened when I said yes to going with him but my thoughts were never set in the aftermath. I imagined him asking me to be his girlfriend after we had sex. It pains me having to go through a pain like this.

Time went by. I needed a distraction, I needed to stop feeling sorry for what I did. Work and school kept me busy but I needed to pick different hobbies for myself in my free time to occupy my thoughts that kept going back and forth in deciding whether I should send him a message to yell at him or something.

Chapter 3 : The Gamer

Lucia

I kept getting ads on social media about this virtual game online, so I decided to try it. I noticed that playing online made me get away from my problems. It kept my mind busy. It actually made me very good at the game which got me invited to play online with other people. I started chatting with people online and became good friends with this guy that had a smooth, deep but comforting voice. His name is Cole. I started spending all of my free time with Cole playing online games. He made me laugh, made it feel safe. He became my online best friend. It's hard to describe but he has been the only person until now to make me feel the way I do. I don't want to put my hopes up because I might never meet him in real life. Looking up his profile I sent him a quick message.

"Cole, what time are you getting online?"

Hoping he would respond quickly because he was the only person that would make me feel happy when I was feeling down.

"Hi Lucia, I will be going online soon, I'll send you an invite" Cole responded.

I waited for him to get online. I put on my headset, his deep voice always made me feel something in the pit of my stomach. We both spent hours playing and talking. We got so used to it that it became a routine. Cole got more relaxed as time passed, he started calling me his virtual gamer girlfriend. We would text each other outside the game too which I did not intend for our text to turn in a different direction but as time went by we kind of flirted. We shared more private conversations.

"Cole, how old are you?"

Was one of the questions I asked the first time we got to messaging privately.

"How old are you?" he said.

"Hey, I asked you first"

He was deflecting the question so it made me think that he was older than me, I also kind of knew because his voice made me think otherwise.

"Lucia, if I tell you, I have a feeling you will not like me anymore." Cole said.

I started getting anxious,

"Don't worry about that, please tell me. I promise not to get mad"

He responded right away,

"I am forty three years old, how old are you Lucia? I think I can guess how old you are but it's best not to assume."

I knew he was older but never thought there was this much of an age gap between us.

"I'm about to be twenty two years old in a few months, how old did you think I was?"

" I kind of had a feeling you were in your twenties"

After that set of messages and more private conversations.

We asked each other about our previous relationships, he was brief with his response while I told him everything that I went through.

"Lucia, can I ask you a question?"

"Yeah sure, what's your question?"

" Would you ever want to meet in person? I know we both live in the same state so i feel like it would be easy to meet up"

The first month of us playing online games together he had asked me what state I was living in, after I had confirmed that I lived in the same state as him, I also told him that we were only a couple of hours away after he confirmed his exact location. He must have been thinking about this question for a while. I had already experienced saying "yes" impulsively to Eddy and now Cole was asking me something similar and I did not want to get my heartbroken again but I also didn't want to say "no" because what if I just need to live in the moment and have fun without getting my heart in the way. I knew that was impossible for me, I always think with my heart. I was scared, I had never seen him before. Yes, his voice might be super sexy and probably might be good looking but I still needed to be careful. I need to make sure I cover all my tracks before agreeing to something I might regret again.

"Cole, I don't even know what you look like? Maybe if I knew what your face looks like then I might give you an answer"

"I can send you a picture if that's what you are looking for?"

I was curious so I accepted. He sent the picture. He was very good looking and did not look like he was in his forties.

"I would be happy to meet you in person" the message was sent without any real thought.

"How about I pay for your gas to drive half way, I'll meet you the other half. We can go eat, talk and walk around the mall?

I knew I was probably making another mistake by meeting up with someone I only knew a few months but I was tired of being lonely, I was tired of not living in the now, not having fun. I didn't care, I was seeking attention, I wanted to feel loved, to be taken care of. I am guessing this comes from my long term impact of not having a paternal figure in my life.

"My father was barely there for me, he left when I was four years old. While my mom was fighting custody of me, the court had decided I could have visits from time to time. I would only visit him once or twice a month. He was never my first love. He never taught me anything."

A father is supposed to set the standards for his baby girl for when she grows up to find the love of her life. He was supposed to be a role model, a father figure, the person I could come to when I got my heart broken, this was never provided by him. I did have my mother who was always there to bring me back up when I felt down but I don't think it's the same feeling. Instead all I got growing up was him manipulating me, insulting me, making comments about how I'm just like my mother. Every conversation growing up ended in a fight which now I can see that it was toxic. I tried to give him the chance to change, and my mother allowed me to have a relationship with him because she wanted me to come to my own conclusion on how my father was as a person. I understand her point, but I feel it would've been better to never have had that growing up because he made me sick.

In the end I decided to accept Cole's invitation. I drove 2 hours away and he drove 2 hours as well to meet me halfway. When I got there, we both needed to park at the mall. He got out of his car the minute he saw me pull up. I turned the car off and opened my door. He hugged me so hard that he was taking my breath away. His close proximity made me hot and bothered. He made me nervous that I could feel my legs shake.

"Hi Cole-" he did not even let me finish because his lips were on mine.

I tilted my head to deepen the kiss. I felt all the sparks and butterflies in that minute of him kissing me. Once he pulled away, our eyes met then he spoke first–

"I'm sorry, I didn't even ask you if this was okay"

"It's okay, I liked it. It just took me by surprise."

His smile was so irresistible, I was happy I had made the decision to meet up with him.

We walked hand in hand to the nearest food place. After we got seated, we looked over the menu to order some food. When we got done with our food we walked around the mall until we were tired.

"Lucia, I want to ask you to stay at least one more day so we can hang out tomorrow too."

"Cole, where am I going to stay? I didn't book a hotel" I uttered loudly.

"I kind of booked one for you to stay, I had a feeling that we needed more time together." Cole murmured.

The memories came rushing in from my time with Eddy. Will this time be different? Will I get my forever person? Will he be different with me after I give him what he clearly wants from me?

"Where will you stay Cole?" I hesitated.

"I could stay with you if you don't mind or If you don't feel comfortable sharing a bed with me I can drive out here again tomorrow"

I was starting to sweat. It felt like I already made many mistakes with men. I didn't want to turn down this opportunity.

I haven't had sex in a long time and I was already feeling something between my legs with that kiss he gave me.

I counted to 100 in my mind and said fuck it! I stepped in front of him tugging his shirt,

"Cole, I want you to stay with me, it will be nice to wake up to you in the morning. We can hang out all day tomorrow before i head back home"

He was absolutely delighted by my response that he carried me, hooking my legs around his waist. He spun me around in circles letting out all his emotions he was feeling. We drove our cars to the hotel he had chosen. Got checked in, the room was nice and clean. As he closed the door, I went to freshen up in the bathroom. I'm thankful that I shaved the day before as a just in case moment. I splashed some water on my face, dried off and walked back to the room. Cole was waiting for me sitting down on the edge of the bed. Walking towards him, he grabs me by my hand pulling me in between his legs. Grabbing my waist leaning in for a hug then pulled back to look me in the eyes. As we made eye contact, he laced his fingers together behind my neck bringing me lower so my lips met his. His mouth was on mine. That's all it took for me to become wild in heat. I was on cloud nine when he started to undress me. It took a total of 5 seconds for our lips to part ways when he got my shirt off me. Then his lips were back on mine.

"Lucia, (kiss)you are (kiss) so beautiful. I can't (kiss)believe you are here (kiss)with me in this (kiss)very moment"

Cole was delicate and took his time as a true gentleman. He knew what I needed. I have always been conscious about my body, I've never been a skinny girl. I was always on the thicker side. He made me feel good about my body when he reassured me by having his hands all over my ass and tits. I lay down in bed, he lowered my pants down along with my panties. Once naked I covered myself. This time he reassured me again with words.

"Lucia, don't ever do that! Don't ever cover yourself in front of me. I love your body"

Uncovering myself he gave me kisses from my ankle all the way up to my inner thigh.

Breathless he said,

"It's this okay? Should I go slower?"

"I just haven't had anyone down there before" I said nervously.

"It's okay baby, I'll take care of you. I'll make you feel real good. I'll show you what no one has ever shown you before and I'm glad that I am your first." Cole said.

"I'm not a virgin, I just meant that you are the first to go down on me"

He made his way in between my legs and parted them with his knees. Started to lower himself until my legs were wide open. The first lick was magical, had me caving with all the feelings.

"Oh my god! That feels so good!"

Using his fingers to open me up, working his tongue inside me. He pushed a finger inside while he kept on licking me between my folds. It was the first time someone had gone down on me and it was so perfect.

"Cole is too sensitive but it feels so good."

I came twice. He brought himself up to kiss me and I could taste myself. Grabbing his wallet from the nightstand, he took out a condom. Tore the packet up, he took out the condom with one hand while lowering his pants and boxers with the other hand. Slid the condom on his cock then positioned himself to push his cock inside me. I've never seen a cock this big, it was bigger than my first. This felt different too, he took his time to pleasure me first. Cole took care of me while he pleasured himself. We did it two times in two different positions. He was a gentleman, he cleaned me up after we were done and sleep took over us from exhaustion. It was so much better than I expected.

"The next day was a shit show. I was let down AGAIN!"

When I woke up, he was not in bed. I heard his voice coming from the bathroom as if he was on the phone. I did not want to intrude but I was curious as to who he was talking to, this early in the morning. I got up, tiptoed towards the bathroom. That's when I overheard, *"No babe, I just woke up. I did not see your text messages from yesterday night. I will be home later today. I am working the whole morning."*

Wait- what? my mind racing whispering to myself "What the fuck is going on?" as I put my ear against the door to be able to hear what he was saying. I was still whispering to myself "Damn, he has a girlfriend! He just cheated on her with me!" I put two and two together — he had to be a man in a relationship. All I could think was,

" I just had sex with a married man!"

I started to shiver, It wasn't even cold. It was just my body reacting to the guilt, disappointment and embarrassment. My legs were giving up on me. At this very moment I was wishing I could go back in time where I didn't accept his invitation. I was about to hit a wall, and he still needed to come out of the bathroom to confirm all of my suspicions.

Chapter 4 : Cheater, Cheater

Lucia

As Cole finished his phone conversation, I tiptoed back to where my clothes were. I got dressed then shoved the rest of my things inside my purse. I was getting nauseous, a protruding headache was developing. All I wanted to do was get out of there without getting any explanation.

"Fuck that! I need an explanation. I deserved it!"

Cole unlocked the bathroom door, his gaze went straight to me since I was awake and already standing at the edge of the bed dressed. He saw the killing stare I was giving him then he knew he had fucked up!

"Let me explain– I know you might be mad, probably want to scream at me or punch me but I have an explanation for all of this" Cole said.

"Go ahead because right now I have no idea what the fuck is going on"

I gave him the chance to explain, I did not want to leave upset and drive like this.

"Look Lucia, the reason why i didn't tell you anything about me being married, is because I knew you would not want anything with me"

"Damn right! Fuck!" I yelled.

"My wife and I are not on good terms, we haven't been good for a while now and you were there to pick me up, bring me happiness when I was going through it with my wife"

"Cole, you should've been honest with me from the beginning. How do you expect me to react when we just had sex and I just found out you are married!"

"I know—I know— I'm sorry. I like you a lot, I don't want this to end." he was stuttering nervously, by the look on his face he was devastated he got caught. I sat down on the chair that was next to a small table. I stared into space quietly for a while contemplating what I was going to do. Then he took a step forward and then another until he was right in front of me. I lifted my hand to stop him but he still cupped my face tilted my chin,

"Ask me anything, I'll be honest this time"

I took on his offer asking him all the questions I needed to feel more at ease, even though I knew it wouldn't work. The more I asked the more I felt I needed to take a step back. My mind was full of questions, doubts, insecurities and guilt. I had to ask the last burning question that kept creeping up on me,

"Cole, would you leave your wife for me?" murmured, afraid of his answer.

He looked into my eyes, his eyes desperately told me the answer. knowing that he was going to say "no." He hesitated to answer with a frustrated sigh,

"I've never really thought about that." He explained that they don't have kids together and that his wife has health issues.

"Men never leave their wives! and you are not going to be the exception!"

I got up, grabbed my purse and I turned towards the door to leave. He tried to stop me by putting his body in between the door and I.

"Sorry, I can't deal with this right now. I need time and space" he stepped to the side letting me go. Once out the door I paused for a second to take in what really happened. Went straight to my car without turning back. Driving the two hours back home devastated, I did not shed a tear. Tired of crying and feeling sorry for myself every time I choose wrong or make a mistake.

"What will people think of me? What is my mother going to think of me, my family?"

I did not want anyone to find out about this. I didn't tell a soul, so I wouldn't be judged. I couldn't stop thinking about his wife though, I felt sorry for her. For having a husband that cheated on her. Knowing that she has health issues, he probably got tired of being a caregiver I don't know... I took some time off from playing online. I couldn't talk to him. Cole sent me multiple messages asking if I was back home. If I was planning to play online or even talk to him again. I did not reply back, that just meant falling back into a vicious circle where I'm the second option.

"The other women, the mistress"

Even though I did not cry about this situation, I was still going through it. I got depressed, I lost the only friend I had that made me happy. I just wanted Cole back. He made me feel loved, I needed him but I knew I couldn't go back and betray my morals. Weeks went by, I had not played online for weeks but today I felt a little braver. Turning on the game I got a private chat invite from Cole. I accepted the request needing closure. I knew what I had to do. This was going to be my last chat.

"Hi"

He swallowed hard, adjusting his headset before saying "hi". It was the most awkward chat

"Lucia please forgive me, I never wanted to put you in this situation, I genuinely care for you. You are my best friend. I don't really have a large group of friends. You made me happy any time you got online or even just messaged me."

"Cole, you're married. We can't do this. I can only be your friend, it's your only choice. I am not going to let you cheat on your wife, you know damn well that you are not planning on divorcing her to be with me"

"Lucia, how could I think of divorcing her when she still needs me, she is sick! She doesn't have anyone else but me. Look at me, I am forty three years old, you are in your twenties. I don't want to take your opportunity from growing up having an actual boyfriend, maybe a husband, kids, and everything else your future may hold. I guess, at the moment when I invited you to meet me, I wasn't thinking clearly. I never thought you would say yes to meeting me. It was in the heat of the moment that I booked the hotel and asked you to stay. I did not want to hurt you but I wanted to feel loved since it's been a while."

His words broke me, when he spoke the usual happiness he had was gone. His strained tone made my own chest hurt understanding him a little bit more.

"Cole, I understand everything. I am not judging you for the way you went about things. Maybe at first but now that I have more context I can say that I get it. We just can't do this to your wife. I don't want to be your second option, I don't want to be anyone's second option."

"Lucia I would like to keep you as a friend if you don't mind. I know it will be hard on us because we have so much chemistry but I don't really want to lose you" after that request, I basically just went with it for that day but I did not get online after that. I needed to take a step back and figure out what I wanted to do with everything. When I did, I came to the conclusion that I should stay away from any temptation and do what was right. Cole and I stopped talking to each other. I managed to keep going with my life as planned. I graduated from college and got enrolled into the closest university to get my bachelors. Classes started and I became extremely busy trying to get good grades.

Out of the bloom I started connecting back with Tatiana. She invited me out on weekends, I took her invitation with the hope of taking my mind off of things. I also started to connect more with friends that I used to talk to from high school. I got promoted to full time at work while being part time at the university. I was living at home with my mother and stepdad still to keep on saving money. I was the number one top seller of the month at work and I was proud of myself. I was starting to feel a little better from everything that I had gone through. Since I couldn't play online, I took on other things as a hobby to clear my mind. I started working out whenever I felt stressed. I took on painting, coloring, and crafts in my free time. I also started making videos on social media of me cooking which brought me joy. For some time, I was happy but got bored of the routine. I hated not having someone to share my adventures or accomplishments. I was sure I would be single forever. I wasn't meeting anyone worth my time. No one I could trust. I was adamant but I needed to learn to love myself. I promised myself to not look for love. I needed to start enjoying life being single. Go on adventures and celebrate accomplishment even if I couldn't share them with a special partner.

"I should be more than enough!"

I stopped looking at my past and the guilt I put myself through for making bad decisions.

Chapter 5 : The Set Up

Lucia Present day

The year started with big changes. I dyed my hair burgundy red. I wanted something new and something out of my comfort zone. I received many compliments, it made me feel so good about myself. My red hair complimented my caramel skin tone. I felt adventurous so I got my lip pierced. I took my mother on a trip just the two of us and we had so much fun. I was accomplishing my goals. My life was going great then suddenly our family dog passed away. It was so painful to grief our family pet. We had him for over 10 years. He was our baby. I had to go through this while I was still in school and working. I was preparing for exams to graduate soon. Work kept me busy full time. All of a sudden my phone starts to beep. I take it out of my pockets,

"Ping"— My phone beeped again. It was a private message.

" Hey Lucia, How are you? Have you seen my sister? Is she with Jessica?" -Daniels

It was a friend from high school. I remember him from my math class. His sister hangs out a lot with my cousin who also lives with me. I'm guessing he can't get in touch with his sister so his best contact is me.

"Hey Daniels, no I have not seen your sister. I will text Jessica to see if they are together and I'll get back to you" I replied back.

I called Jessica and asked her if she was with Barbara.

"Lucia, tell him to stop being so protective of Barbara and let her have fun. We are not doing anything wrong." Jessica responds.

"Just tell her to call her brother so he is not worried okay."

I replied back to Daniels telling him that they are together and that Barbara will call him soon. Then I got a reply back immediately,

"Lucia, how have you been? We haven't seen each other since high school. I remember back when we used to have class together."

I did not want to lead him into talking back and forth and for him to think I was interested. I am doing well at staying focused and I didn't want to get hurt again by talking to someone from high school. I also didn't want to be rude so my response was short.

"I've been good, yes it's been a long time since high school."

He seemed to understand my short response because there was no response. A week passed by, a message on my social media appeared from him. The message conveyed the need for my personal number because he needed to contact me urgently. I messaged him quickly with a sense of uncertainty. Not even a minute later, my phone started to ring.

"Ring"

"Ring"

"Hello"

"Lucia, sorry to call but I just needed someone to talk to about Jessica and Barbara"

Chuckling on the inside because this man wants to talk about his sister and my cousin.

"You scared me you idiot, I thought something happened" we both laughed out loud.

"No, I'm just tired that my sister and your cousin are always up to no good and it's making my mom worried and then I get sent to do my big brotherly duty which is to take care of her."

"No worries, I get it. It's the same with me and my cousin. I'm always the one taking care of her so I understand perfectly." We talked for hours reminiscing about everything we did in high school. We also talked about the mischievous things his sister did with my cousin. When we hung up, it must have been hours of us just talking. The next day he sent me a message again.

"WYD? (what you doing)"

"I'm just at home watching TV"

Then his next message was him complementing my new picture I posted to my social media. The one of me showing my new red hair with my lip piercing. Just as we were messaging he asked me a question that left me silent because I was not expecting this question from him. We never really talked about intimate things or asked each other about our relationship status.

"Lucia, are you still single" Knowing where this conversation was going, I hesitated to answer but still gave an answer to get it out of the way.

"Yeah, I'm still single. Not really looking though. I have too much on my plate at the moment"

What came after took me by surprise though– he was most

certainly not asking for himself. It was for someone else.

"I have someone that might be interested in you."

Puzzled, because he is trying to hook me up with a friend! Why?

"I'm curious why you want to set me up with a friend of yours"

"It looks to me that you might need someone in your life to share all your accomplishments. Someone who truly loves you for who you are. Someone who will treat you right."

Wondering if Jessica had said something to Barbara and then Barbara told her brother something about me being cheated on before and my little mistake with Eddy? I know she couldn't have told her about Cole because that part of me has stayed sealed. Was he feeling pity for me? or was he genuinely trying to set me up with a good person? In the end, he ended up telling me that Barbara was told by Jessica what I have been through and how sad I was.

"So who is this person you want to set me up with?"

I didn't go looking for this I swear, I wasn't planning on going out with anyone. I've been single for a long time but It wouldn't hurt to open up my heart again, maybe the third time is my lucky charm. I need to face my fears and see where it takes me.

"My friend saw your profile picture while I was scrolling through our messages and he said that you were really cute and really liked your red hair." Daniels said.

Rosy-cheeked, thanking God he couldn't see me behind the screen.

"How old is he? What does he do for a living and how well do you know him?"

"He is a year older than you. He is hardworking and I know him very well. We have been friends for years. He is a decent guy"

Mm... okay he is twenty five years old, hardworking, decent

guy. Okay! Sold!

"Do you have a picture of him?"

"Unfortunately, he is very reserved. He doesn't post much on social media. Barely has any pictures. So are you interested?"

"Why not! Lucia, what do you have to lose? Go for it!" That's what my little brain kept telling me.

"Sure, tell him to add me on social media first and we can see from there."

It didn't take long for his friend to add me on social media. I accepted the request and we began to message each other right away. I was so eager to get to know him. It's been a while since I talked to someone that is interested in me. I kept scrolling, scrolling through his page to see if he had any pictures. I was going crazy because I wanted to see what he looked like. Then I opened the message he had sent.

"Hey, my name is Julian Vega. I'm hoping Daniels already told you all about me. I wanted to message you directly to tell you that you are beautiful. Your red hair is extraordinary. I wanted to reach out so we can get to know each other, if that's okay with you."

I was already starting to blush, it was the second time that I got a beautiful compliment about my red hair. Being bold and brave I replied back,

"Thank you, I wish I could call you handsome but I haven't seen any pictures of you on social media. Daniels told me a little bit about you but I'm looking forward to knowing you more."

We had so many messages going back and forth, asking each other things you ask when you start dating someone. I learned what he does for a living. He works a lot of hours which sucks because that might be an issue with my schedule. He said that he is an extrovert and easily makes friends. We messaged each other for two weeks straight. He told me that he was going to take me out soon so we could meet in person.

"Can I take you to dinner and a movie?"

I was jumping up and down like a lunatic from happiness,

"Of course, what do you have in mind and when?"

"How about tomorrow at 7pm and we can go watch a scary movie."

"That sounds good. I will meet you at the restaurant. Just give me the details when you have something planned out." I wanted to take my own car just in case I needed to run. I burst into laughter thinking about running.

"Good but next time I am driving you there. I'll meet you at the restaurant. Can't wait to meet you!"

"Wait– How am I supposed to know who you are when I don't know what you look like?"

I knew he was replying back because the three dots appeared and then disappeared multiple times as he was deciding what to say. I assumed he would send me a picture of himself but the fucker said,

I guess you will have to find out tomorrow"

There is no way! I will go in blindsided, feeling the tension because I did not want to feel disappointed. I'm not the type of person to judge someone by their looks but I also was curious to see him face to face. The next day couldn't have come any faster. It was 6:30 pm. I showered, waxed and straightened my hair. Yes! You heard right "waxed". I am not expecting anything sexual on the first date! But you can't ever be too sure. Right?

I wore blue jeans that hugged my ass just right, picked a brown and gold blouse with a cozy brown jacket with fur on top. I picked my favorite perfume, purse and shoes. I stepped inside my car putting the heater on because I was freezing my ass, it was 40 degrees. It took me 20 minutes to get to the restaurant. I parked my car at the nearest open space outside the restaurant, the time on the dash pointed to 6:50 pm. I took one last look in the mirror before heading out to the entrance of the restaurant. Sat my ass down on the bench of the waiting area. I messaged him letting him know I was already here.

There's a first time for everything, This blind date was a first for me! I needed to compose myself, I was nervous! Then there he was! Walking in like he owns the place. He opened the door standing at the entrance, gazing left and right to find me. When another couple started to move in to get seated, he saw me! I felt as if I was in slow motion. He moved from the entrance taking a step towards me. Something inside me told me "this is him", and in that moment I knew in my heart that this gorgeous man in front of me is Julian Vega.

My Julian Vega!

Chapter 6 : Blind Date

Lucia

He was right in front of me. We silently stared into each other's eyes. I couldn't talk, I felt as if I was going to stutter or something because the man right in front of me is so handsome, he smells so good and is very well dressed.

"Lucia, are you surprised? — because I am! Your pictures are beautiful but you in person wow! You're gorgeous."

I decided to get up from the bench to give him a hug. Everything about him was melting my insides, he smelled so good. I don't know what cologne he is using but I want to devour him. We got seated by the window. With our menus in hand we chose our food then got to talking. I was hoping there would be no awkwardness between us in fact there wasn't any because our conversation was flowing naturally. Knowing that I am an introvert sometimes it's hard to engage with people but with Julian it seemed to be going quite alright.

Chapter 6 : Blind Date

"So, tell me how has your week been? I know we haven't messaged much because of work. Anything interesting?"

"It's been good just work and school, pretty busy as well. How about you?"

"It's been good, busy too. I've been dying for this day. All I wanted was for this day to happen so I could get to know you more personally."

"Yes me too, hit me with any question you have." I said it too excitedly.

"What are you looking for in a guy?"

"Well, I want a man that can make me laugh, who is kind,loyal, who loves me for who I am, who is responsible, someone I can share my accomplishment with, someone I can talk to and confide as a best friend. What about you?"

"Good, I'm wanting exactly the same. I want a girl that will be uplifting me. Standing next to me while I accomplish my goals, I want to have adventures and journeys together in the future. How many serious relationships have you had?" He asked.

"I haven't really had a serious relationship, I have had a couple of boyfriends here and there but nothing really serious since high school. And you?"

"To be completely honest, I have only been with two girls in the past . One was not serious and the other one was but that ended because she cheated on me. Look, I want to be straight with you about this because this is the reason why I haven't been in a relationship in a long time. The cheating really messed me up. I don't cheat, in fact I hate people lying and cheating. Once a person loses my trust, I am never giving it back."

Getting cheated on was painful and it messes with your head because you try to think what it is that you did that made them do that, then you question yourself if you aren't enough for that person.

"I get it, I am the same. This is the only thing I ask from my partner "loyalty". I was cheated on as well and I don't want to go through that again either.

Our server got to our table asking if we were ready to order, I ordered Carbonara pasta with water and he ordered a steak with mashed potatoes with a doctor pepper. The food was delicious. We both were feeling confident with all the things we had shared about each other. We stared into each other's eyes, we both could see that we had lots of chemistry. He kept gawking at me while we were waiting for our server to come back with the check. Once the bill was paid, we stood up from our table, walked hand in hand to our cars. He asked me if it was okay for him to drive me to the movie theater. He clarified that he will drive me back here to my car afterwards. He opened the door to his car to let me in. Being a gentleman was making my stomach feel tingly. I just met him and all of these feelings were making me fall for him. Yes, a hopeless romantic, I always put my heart and feelings first when meeting someone which is painful when they hurt you in the end. Inside his car he reached for my hand to intertwine together. He asked, "It's this okay?" I nodded like an idiot because I was falling so hard. I was having a great time, I didn't want this day to end. We got to the theater's parking lot, he parked his car and waited a little before getting out. Turning off the car he pivoted to check me out and said "you are so beautiful".

I was trying not to breathe too hard so that he couldn't see how nervous he was making me feel. A burning, melting feeling spreading in my stomach then into my chest that's what I was feeling. He opened my door, extending his hand to mine. He intertwined his fingers with mine again as we walked towards the theater. My smile was from cheek to cheek just seeing us walk hand in hand making me look like his girlfriend. I know I was about to make an impulse decision but decided to leave it for the end of our blind date. We got our tickets, our snacks and sat down in our assigned seats. The movie was scary and it justified the way he pulled me into his side to hug me, then he rested his hand on my leg throughout the entirety of the movie. Once the movie finished, we began to walk our way to the exit to go to his car. He drove me back to my car within minutes. I needed to make my move before leaving. The time is running out.

"If we were in a movie, then this is the time where the girl gets her kiss from her prince charming". I wasn't getting any clues or hints that he was going to kiss me but I get it he is probably trying to be respectful and not cross the line. I wanted to kiss him though. Taking all of those fears I had, I stepped in front of him and got close to him. I softly said to him,

"I hope you don't take this the wrong way"

Moving another inch into his personal space, then I gave him a kiss. It was a quick and cute little peck. With broken words and a nervous laugh he said,

"Wow— thank you for that. I really wanted to kiss you but I didn't want you to feel uncomfortable or think I was moving too fast. I haven't felt that in a long time and I really liked that."

With a grin from cheek to cheek I placed both my hands on his cheeks. I needed to catch my breath but I was still able to say, "I would really like to go out on a second date with you if you like? I hope you don't think I was moving fast too. I kissed you because I felt our chemistry throughout our whole date and I knew you were trying to be respectful but I needed that kiss to prove myself that what I'm feeling for you right now is real? Please tell me I was not the only one feeling that?" I said.

"I would love to take you on a second date Lucia, I really enjoyed our date and of course I don't take the kiss the wrong way. I was being a gentleman, I did not want to make you uncomfortable but I definitely wanted to kiss you tonight so many times, I am so glad you did." he said.

He gave me a hug so tight that it felt as if he never wanted to leave my side,

"Please message me when you get home safe and I will figure out a plan for our second date. I'll send you the details okay."

"Thank you again for the perfect date. I'll send you a message as soon as I get home, drive safe as well." I said.

I got in my car, strapped my seat belt. Took a long breath but it wasn't enough to calm my nerves. My heart was going miles per hour with what just happened. I couldn't think straight. I still backed away from the parking space, looking back in my mirror I saw him getting inside his car. As I was driving on the road, I could not stop smiling and feeling all the things a girl is supposed to feel when she is falling for someone. Call me crazy or an idiot but in this exact moment I believed in love at first sight, It's real! You won't believe in it unless you experience it first hand. I fell head over heels for this man not even knowing him. It's been a couple of hours since we met, and I'm already in love.

I never thought that this man would swoop me off my feet to make me feel something I haven't felt before. This was more intense than what I felt with Cole. I think with Cole, it was more about the idea of having someone that I wanted their attention, maybe someone that made me feel good about myself but it was never about love. Reminding myself that what I felt for Cole was nothing compared to what I feel for Julian. Cole lied to get what he wanted, the age gap was a bit concerning now that I think about it and everything would've been a mess because I know my whole family would have judged me. I know for damn sure my mother would've been horrified by my actions, she would have said she didn't raise me that way.

Feeling like nothing could stop me from this happiness, I went through my days with no care in the world. That is what Julian was making me feel. I prayed every night letting God know that he needed to take care of me. To please keep me out of harm's way. I kept repeating to myself hoping that I wasn't going to be let down once again so I prayed every night. Julian didn't wait long to text me with his plan for the second date. He texted me while i was at school,

"Lucia, are you free on Saturday night? I have the perfect plan to go for our second date."

"Hey, mmm.. What do you have planned? And yes, I am free Saturday night " I replied back.

"Well, It's a surprise, just like how we met. I want to pick you up this time though. Send me your address and I'll pick you up around 5 pm if that's okay with you?" He said.

"Yes of course, that sounds like a plan. I'm excited, can't wait to see you."

I was so excited for our second date because not only I get to see him again but maybe kiss again, I can't wait to spend our time together. Saturday couldn't come any faster, I was trying to see what I wanted to wear. I decided on jeans, a nice blouse with a denim jacket and my checkered vans. I started getting ready for our second date 2-3 hours before the actual pick up time. I showered, waxed, and for the first time I let my natural curly hair down because I didn't want to take hours straightening it. I was ready by 4:45 pm and waited seated on my couch.

“Ping”

“Ping” my phone beeped inside my purse.

“I’m outside” Julian’s message appeared on my phone.

I got out the front door without looking back because I knew my mother was looking through the window to see the guy I was going out on a second date with. Julian got out of his car once he saw me. Opening the passenger door for me,

“What a gentleman”

“I try to be but for you I’ll do it forever”

There I go again blushing like a tomato because he said “FOREVER” and that meant a lot to me.

“So, where are you taking me?”

“Patience my lady” He said, grinning hard. Pulling out of my house, he began to drive to the destination he planned to have for our second date.

Chapter 7 : Our Chemistry

Lucia

We got to this cute miniature golf place about 30 minutes from my house. It felt so nice to enjoy time with him again. I didn't know how to play miniature golf so I was hoping for him to guide me just like how I saw in movies, with his hands on my waist showing me how to swing the golf club because I enjoyed his close proximity so much. We played, laughed, blushed, and enjoyed our second date. By the time we were done, he asked me if I was hungry. Of course I said yes, I was starving myself because I did not want to be full or bloated by the time he picked me up.

"Where do you want to go eat or should I pick?"

"Would you mind if we pick a drive thru and eat in the car? I don't want to share you with people right now if that's okay with you?. I just want it to be us." Biting my lips, he saw right through me, he knew what I wanted.

"I don't mind, where do you have in mind?" he said.

"Are you okay with burgers?"

"I'm down for burgers, I'll look for the closest location"

He drove to the best burger place, then we ate in the car. There was a lot of talking, lots of staring back and forth and a lot of kissing too. By the time we were finished, he gathered the things that needed to be thrown away. Back in the car he could not stop staring at my lips.

"Mm you have something right here–" he took his calloused fingers and swiped the sauce off my lips.

I could hear my own gulp. I was going to thank him but without another word, he kissed me once more. The kiss was like fireworks. Nothing else existed outside these doors. He leaned more to kiss my cheeks, then my neck and went back to my lips. He grabbed my face with those very large hands and made me look at him closely. I could hear his heartbeat, he was about to say something but I cut him off.

"Wow" I didn't know how to breathe like a normal person. I wanted to tell him I loved him already. My heart was going to explode with everything I was feeling in that very moment.

Julian

Since the very first blind date, I could say that this woman was very interesting. She caught my attention. I never thought I would be liking another girl since I swore I was done with relationships. Everything I went through with my last relationship made me think I didn't have a chance at love anymore. When my friend Daniels was going through his account, I was sitting right next to him when I noticed the girl he was talking to on his account. I turned to him and said

"Damn" so loud that everyone stopped what they were doing and turned to me. I guess I had intended to say that in my head but I didn't. Daniels turned to me and said,

"She's pretty right?"

"She's beautiful and that hair wow!" I said

"I can introduce you if you like? She's been my friend since high school. My sister is very good friends with her cousin so we pretty much know each other personally. I'm just gonna go ahead and say it; "She is one of the good ones if you ask me." He knows exactly about my situation on how I got cheated on by my last girlfriend.

I know he is just trying to be a good friend but I don't want him to feel bad for me just because I don't have a girlfriend. I didn't want him to think I wasn't interested either; because I was! I didn't want him to be the one interested in her. Feeling a little protective over her—*what the hell? Why am I being protective of her when I don't even know her!*

"What's her name and how old is she?" I said.

"Her name is Lucia, she is a year younger than you. She works and goes to school full time. I know she is single because I just asked her, I might have told her that I might have a friend interested in her." Daniels said it with a chuckle, like he had been planning this shit.

Bastard, he was already trying to set me up with her without even knowing if I wanted to or not. Let's be real, I wanted to 100 percent.

"So what did she say?" Desperately waiting for him to answer because I didn't want to put my hopes up. I wanted her to say "yes" to at least talking to me; to get to know me. It's been a year since I've had sex with anyone. I didn't just want her for sex, I wanted her because she is beautiful. But if sex it's involved with her then I'll be happier. Daniels didn't need to know about me not having sex in a year. Daniels kept his eyes on his phone while he was messaging her and I was becoming impatient because he just kept messaging back and forth with her without giving me any details. So I bumped his shoulder to ask him,

"Soo.. did she say anything?"

"Yeah, she definitely wants to talk to you. She said to add her on her social media account. You guys can go from there" Daniels was eyeing me with the happiest grin because he wants me to be happy. Knowing that I will fall for someone and put my trust again is going to be difficult but I got to start somewhere. You have to be willing to risk things in life in order to make something happen but I will also always have it in the back of my mind the "what if" if I don't open my heart to this girl.

I sent her the friend request as soon as Daniels told me what she said, from there we had a good conversation. Our first date was nerve wrecking but I really liked playing this little game of her not knowing how I looked. I don't have many pictures on social media and the only picture I had was from many years ago where I had long hair which I don't anymore. As I stepped out of my car to head to the entrance of the restaurant, she sent me a message saying she was on a bench waiting for me. I couldn't see her from where I was so I started fidgeting with my nails as I walked inside. It took me 25 steps to get there, yes! I counted. I was that nervous. As soon as the couple in front of me moved, I saw her, she was on her phone. She looked more beautiful than her pictures. She stood up as we both went in for a hug and damn she smelled so good. It was a fruity citrus smell. Her hair was fiery red, dressed really nice with jeans that made her ass look fabulous. I am an ass type of man!I can't deny it and hers is the most voluptuous ass I have ever seen and I love it.

Once seated we talked about all the things that we were expecting from our future partners, in this case "each other" and we were pretty much in the same train of thought. We finished our food, I paid and then went straight to the movie theater. The movie I picked was on purpose. It was a scary movie, I knew I could bring her close enough to me since she had told me she doesn't really watch scary movies because she is afraid of them. Once back to where her car was parked, we were dreading leaving each other's side. I wanted to kiss her so bad but I didn't in the end because she was the one who stole a kiss from my lips first. A kiss that felt a spark igniting a fire inside me, enveloping my whole body. I wanted to kiss her since I saw her at the restaurant but I wanted to stay respectful and I didn't know if she was going to be okay or not. I'm really glad she took the first step because that kiss was wow! She stepped right in front of me and said she would really like a second date because there is so much chemistry between us. Agreeing with her because I never thought that coming into this date would leave wanting her everywhere on me. I made the right decisions in asking her on a date. We both couldn't contain our happiness as we left the parking lot. When I got home I started to look for any ideas for our second date. I did not want to wait too long but I had to check in with her about our schedules.

I picked mini golf as our second date adventure. I was sure that she didn't know how to play so it gave me a chance to show her by keeping my hands on her at all times. It was a good choice because we both had so much fun. She picked burgers for our meal of choice. My little lady wanted me all to herself.

She asked me if we could eat in the car instead of a restaurant and I am super glad she picked that because I didn't want to share her with an audience either. We shared many kisses in the car. I couldn't contain my erection, she was making my cock hungry for her. It was so hard, I had to pull myself together. I want her to be the one to choose whenever she is ready to be intimate with me. I can't wait to make her my girlfriend because I don't want to share her with anyone. *"There I go again being an overprotective motherfucker! She is not mine! Well YET!"*

I'm not the jealous type but I also don't want to think about her dating anyone else or any men trying to touch what's mine because she is MINE!— *"she just doesn't know it yet"*

It might be too soon to call her that but this is how i am feeling for her. I also don't want to scare her if I go too fast. She is so perfect, my tiny little lady (s*he is tiny compared to my height)* Her caramel skin, curly hair, great body, on the thicker side which is what I am looking forward to when we cuddle. More for me to grab on. I think I'm falling hard for her. I don't know how else to express my feelings but she already has me wrapped around her fingers.

Lucia

After that perfect kiss in the car and the sudden bulge I felt when I was on his lap, It's safe to say that Julian enjoyed our heated moment. He waited until I was inside the house to leave. He told me he needed to get back home because he had to go to work early the next day. I also needed to finish school work. I've been procrastinating. I am so close to graduating. Work has been kicking my ass every single day. We now have a new sales goal that we all need to complete before the month ends which keeps getting lower now that I am too busy daydreaming about my new man. Julian and I message here and there throughout the week. My mom and I started arguing because she keeps telling me not to get distracted with my school work, she knows that I'm dating Julian, she keeps saying he is a distraction. The first thing on her mind is that I'm going to get unfocused on my classes and fail them. I'm so frustrated with her, she hasn't paid any attention to me in a while but now exciting things are happening to me, but she is worried which is making us fight a lot more. Funny how she is so invested now, when she didn't do this back when I was in high school. I wanted to get away from my house with the constant fight I keep having with my mom, it was making it more difficult to stay there. So I texted Julian.

"Hey, what are you doing?"

The 3 dots appeared and disappeared on the phone until I finally got a reply.

"Hey, sorry I've been super busy and don't really have a good connection. I'm at work until 12 am. Why? Is there something going on?"

"Well I'm not feeling so good right now, I've been fighting with my mom, I really don't want to stay here tonight. Is there any chance I can stay with you for today? I know you might think that it's too soon to take me to your place but I just want to be with you. Please—".

"If you don't mind waiting for me until I get off from work, I can pick you up and take you to my place but we need to be really quiet. You know I still live with my parents and siblings. I've been trying to save up to get my own place but haven't really put the work into finding one." He said.

"I don't mind, I just want to be with you. I'll be waiting."

Julian messaged me around 11:50 pm to tell me he was getting ready to leave. My mother was already sleeping and she didn't even hear when I stepped out of the house. Julian parked outside, he grabbed my overnight bag for me and before he opened the car door, he grabbed me by the waist pulling me into him to kiss me. He drove to his place, once we got there I followed him inside. Everything in the house was dark and quiet. His parents and siblings were sleeping. He led me inside his room motioning me to sit down on his bed. He locked his room door to make sure no one was able to come in. I didn't think I would be nervous but my palms started sweating. I sat down on the edge of the bed. He apologized for the clothes that were on the floor. I didn't really care about that because I was there for him not to judge his place. The majority of his room was clean except for the clothes on the floor. Coming up to me, standing in between my legs he lifted his hand up to my chin,

"We should go to bed, It's late. Do you have pajamas or should I give you something of mine to wear" I had put some pajamas in my suitcase but having his clothes didn't sound bad at all.

"Can I have a shirt please"

"no need for pants since this shirt is going to fit you like a dress."

Okay, thankfully I don't need to think about anything else since he just wants to go to sleep, I am 100% sure he is super exhausted from work. I stayed in the room to change while he took his clothes to the bathroom to get changed. Having some privacy is nice but I wanted him to change here so I could see everything he is packing. When he got back in the room, he was shirtless.

"I hope you don't mind but I don't really wear clothes when I sleep because my body gets too hot under the covers, but since you are here I'll make the exception with these pants" giving him my stupid in love smile.

"I don't mind, you could actually sleep however you feel most comfortable. Don't change just because I'm here". After telling him that he got comfortable around me.

"You sure, right? because I'm about to be in just my boxer briefs. You can't take it back okay."

I don't know why the hell I said this to him because he started to take his pants tossing them on the floor leaving himself to be just in his boxers where I could still see the outline of his cock. I was sweating so much, I got up from his bed grabbing the pants that were on the floor. I decided I needed to splash some water on myself before he could clearly see that I am melting away. I left the room and went inside the bathroom that was next to his room. In the bathroom I grabbed some wipes to wipe my underarms, my neck and splashed the water on my face to bring my spiked heat down.

Chapter 8 : Decisions

Lucia

Once back in the room, he could tell I was tense so he tried to change any conversation.

"Do you want to watch TV? Or should we go to bed since it's after 1 am?" I couldn't stop thinking about his darn outline and my gaze kept coming back to his briefs. "Mhm"—clearing his throat I met his eyes. I've been caught!

"I think we should go to sleep, you must be really tired from work."

"Do you want to talk about it? If not, it's totally okay." I'm not sure if he is referring to me looking at his bulge or me fighting with my mom so instead of answering the first one, I just answered the one I thought was appropriate.

"Well, we started fighting about me not focusing on school and then she said that I need to be more responsible. She suggested that maybe I need to start paying rent which I'm okay with but she just caught me off guard because we both said I would save that money so I would be able to pay for other bills."

"It's okay baby, your mom is just worried about you and she probably just wants you to learn how to be responsible for when the time comes when you move out." He moved closer to hug me putting his chin on my head. He kissed my forehead knowing I needed that. Sleep took over for us the minute we closed our eyes. The next morning light peeked in through the window, feeling his warmed body next to me making me confused because I didn't recognize where I was for a moment. I must have been really tired to wake up like this. Moving as slow as possible to not wake him up, but he wrapped his hands on my waist pulling me into him from behind to give my neck kisses. Feeling how hard he was, I gasped, turning my head to look at him. He gave me a naughty grin before pulling me more into him where his cock was nestled in my ass.

"Good morning baby, how did you sleep?"

"Morning, I slept really well actually. I'm guessing all thanks to you for keeping me warm, you were right when you said that your body heat is out of this world."

Now that we were awake I wanted to jump up from bed to the bathroom to brush my teeth. I was more conscious about our mouths being close to each other, I didn't want him to smell my morning breath but it was too late for that because he tossed me on my back. He got on top of me to kiss me.

"No- No! I have morning breath! Go away please—"

tickling me he whispered in my ear "I don't care, come here!"

My emotions were running high, I wanted to voice them out and tell him that I loved him but I stayed quiet because I didn't want to freak him out. We both got changed knowing we had our day already planned. Sadly he has to go back to work and

I have errands to run before going back to school. Before he took me back home he had ordered breakfast burritos for us to eat on the drive to my house. At home my mom stopped me before I went into my room. She yelled at me for not telling her that I hadn't slept home.

"Where the hell did you go and why didn't you tell me you were leaving?"

"I was with Julian, you know the guy I'm dating. I needed my space after our little fight."

She didn't like that but hey! I'm 24 years old, almost 25, and she can't tell me what I can or can't do.

——————

Julian's message appeared on my phone as I was scrolling through my social media account.

"What are you doing sexy ?"

Until now I am noticing how much I need Julian's messages. I am really liking the little nicknames he has for me. His messages keep me entertained and It makes me not miss him miserably when I'm at work or at school. I'm falling hard and I need to tell my heart to slow down.

"Hi cutie, I'm just finishing my homework, then I'm going to bed. How about you ?"

"I miss you so much, I wish I didn't have to be at work right now. I'm leaving soon. Do you want to come back with me to my place again?

"I really wish I could but I have to work early, I also have classes the next day so I won't be able to see you until the weekend."

" I'm sad because I don't think I can sleep alone anymore. You spoiled me! I need you there when I wake up and go to sleep. Can you make a bag so you can head to work from my place? You can

follow me with your car and park your car at my place." It's not that I didn't want to go because I really did want to but Julian still had not talked to his mom about us and I didn't want to overstep by staying there and her still not knowing about me.

"Mm.. Julian, what if your mom or your family sees me leaving in the morning? Do they even know about me? I don't want to give your mom the wrong impression" He knows that I'm just trying to make sure his mom likes me when he does introduce me to her.

"No, I haven't told them yet you're right we should wait. I promise I'll plan something special so I can introduce you to her. Can you maybe come by on Saturday morning so we can hang out? My parents won't be there. I have to ask you something but I can only do it in person. Please say yes."

"Yes, I'll go Saturday. I'm looking forward to meeting your mom. I hope she likes me though."

"Of course, she will love you. Trust me! So I'll see you Saturday okay. In the meantime please text me because I'm going crazy without you."

The uncertainty of what was happening Saturday was making me irritated. I needed to know already what he wanted to question me about. Will he finally ask me to be his girlfriend or will he ask me to have sex with him? I am not a virgin but I think with my previous mistakes I wanted to wait until he asks me to be his girlfriend.

Julian

Tomorrow is Saturday, I'm getting irritated from just thinking of the questions I'm going to ask Lucia. I'm not just asking one but two questions which I'm pretty confident about the first one but not so much about the second one because the second one is a bit rushed. She is probably going to get upset or run for the hill but I just want to put it out there just so she knows that I am serious about her. I also need to make a plan to tell my mom that I have a girlfriend who she will be seeing a lot more at home. I didn't tell my whole family because they could be a pain in the ass. I just need mom to know so Lucia can feel more comfortable coming over. Friday night I pulled my mom to the side when she got home from work to tell her about Lucia, she was so happy for me and I knew she would because she has never seen me this happy. We made a lunch reservation at mom's favorite restaurant so they both can get to know each other.

Saturday morning I woke up to get everything ready. My parents were out for the whole day. My siblings were out as well doing what they usually do. I grabbed my phone from the night stand to text Lucia,

"Let me know when you are on your way, drive safe my lady"

"I am heading out now. See you in a couple of minutes"

(Okay, she is on her way, Julian get yourself together, stop being a pussy and just ask her as soon as she gets here! get it over with.)

I heard Lucia park her car, looking out the window I spotted her next to my car. As she was walking up the stairs to get to my door, I opened it for her. I pulled her in, to give her the hug I desperately needed. Taking a step back to check her out. I grabbed her hand to do a 360 spin because she was wearing another tight ass jeans outlining her peach looking ass, a cute glittery shirt paired nicely with her converse. Her ponytail was pulling my thoughts into the dream I had the other day about her where I wrapped my hands around it from behind while I gave it to her rough—

Chapter 8 : Decisions

"Julian, hello, Julian?"

I must have been daydreaming because I only heard her calling my name after the second time. I pull her hand leading her to the room to get started on asking my questions.

She is so adorable with that lovable smile she gives me any time I have my hands on her. I'm falling hard for this girl and she doesn't even know how much I want to tell her this.

"I'm just going to go ahead and say it because I'm nervous enough that I feel like I'm about to fuck everything up. Are you ready for my first question?" she nodded silently already feeling her sweaty palms "Fuck!"

"Do you want to be my girlfriend?" I asked with the biggest smile I can put on my face.

"Yes, yes I do! Oh my god you scared me for a second!" "So what is the second question?"

"My second question is a bit more life changing but I don't want to scare you. It's okay if you say no but I just want to put it out there because I've been thinking about it for a while now."

"Julian, just spill it! You're scaring me!"

" Okay, Okay, I've been thinking and I want to start looking for apartments and I want you to move in with me." (shit!, she is speechless. Did I ruin it? Fuck! She looks like she is about to cry)

The last thing I want is to scare her off. I know I'm doing this way too fast because I just asked her to be my girlfriend and then moving in together is a big responsibility and commitment. I can't read her face, but by the looks of it she did not like my question?

"Can I think about it before I make a decision? I just want to make sure everything at home will be taken care of when I leave, it's that okay?"

(she said she wants to make sure everything at home will be taken care of once she leaves? She literally just said "yes" to moving in. "YES!")

I told her to take her time, even though I already knew her response to moving in together which made me excited because I had been wanting to leave this house and make one of my own. After asking her my questions, I mentioned to her that we have lunch reservations with my mom. Lucia went back home to change. I picked her up a couple of hours later. My parents were already there waiting for us. My sister was also invited with her boyfriend. When we pulled into the restaurant, I turned to face her but Lucia was pale, white as a ghost. I rubbed both her arms up and down to give her some comfort.

"I feel like your mom is not going to like me!"

"Baby, they are going to love you. Don't worry about anything okay. Let's get inside so I can introduce you as my beautiful girlfriend"

Chapter 9 : Boyfriend

Lucia

Meeting my boyfriend's parents in 3.. 2.. 1.. —Yes, I said BOYFRIEND!

This is the happiest I've ever been. I deserve to be happy after everything that I had to overcome this year. When he asked me to be his girlfriend, it was just so perfect. I can't wait to show him off. He is mine and I am his. When he asked me to be his girlfriend, I never thought he would ask me to move in with him but he did. I haven't told him my answer but I already know that I'm going to say yes.

The reservation to the restaurant where I'm meeting Julian's parents is right in front of me. I'm a bit frightened and timid to meet them. I've never really met anyone's parents before so this is a first for me. Julian also invited his younger sister because he thinks It will make me more calmer to know it's not just his parents but since his sister is around my age, I'll be able to feel more comfortable. As we get to the table they are seated,

Julian introduces me to everyone as his girlfriend. I don't even know why I was so frightened about this. His mom and dad are the funniest people I've met. His mom was extremely nice and his sister immediately made me feel comfortable around her. Before leaving the restaurant, Julian's mom pulled me to the side to thank me for making his boy the happiest he has ever been. It made my heart a little sad because I know Julian deserves it since he has been through a lot. He never really had that special person for him and I promise myself to be that person for him.

Everyone was welcoming. Julian took me back home but before he left he told me,

"I can't wait to be able to see you again baby. I'm going to miss you so much. I don't want to be away from you anymore, please think about moving in with me so we get to spend all of our days together."

I took a couple of days to really think about my decision but not because I was afraid but because I needed to plan and figure out the easiest way to tell my mom without hurting her. This is a huge life changing decision, I've never lived on my own and this is a new experience that I wouldn't dare to pass up the opportunity. I want to be able to grow and learn to take care of myself and this will be the perfect way. It's time for me to spread my wings and learn to fly on my own, but in this case it will be with my boyfriend.

"Ma, I just want to tell you how thankful I am for always being there for me, for every advice, for the financial help I received from you to help pay for bills and I cannot tell you how grateful I am to call you my mother." I was tearing up with so many emotions in my heart. She knew this moment was coming,

"I'm moving out soon, I am not sure when but I will let you

know once I find an apartment. I know you might get mad at my decision but I really want to experience this." She started sobbing. It was breaking my heart.

"Don't worry about me, I want you to be happy. I do hope you visit me whenever you can." She left for her room after that.

I went to my room to message Julian.

"Hey, are you working? Can I come over? We need to talk."

"I"m not working today, I'm at a friend's house. You can come over around 5 pm if that's okay? Is it bad news?"

"No, It's not bad news. I'll see you there at 5 pm."

Julian

By 5 pm, I was already back home waiting for Lucia. My mood had changed at my friend's house because I just felt as if Lucia was going to give me bad news. I feel it in my heart that she is not moving in with me, I can't blame her though. It's a big commitment for both of us. At home, my mom had served me a plate of food. I heard Lucia's car when she used her key fob to lock it. When I saw her at the entrance of my house, her face was puffy, she had red eyes and was a little pale. I wrapped her up in a hug.

"Are you okay baby? Have you been crying? Look at your puffy beautiful eyes mi amor (my love)." she nodded with her gaze towards the floor. I hugged her as tight as I could because I know that's what she needs right now. Refusing to eat anything she asked, "Can we go in the room to talk please." she continued,

"Baby, the reason for my visit today is because I want to let you know that I am going to move in with you but you need to promise to make me the happiest woman in this world. This is a big step for me. I want to be able to do this and many other things with you. All I ask is that you don't break my heart and make me regret my decision, okay."

"Yes baby, I promise you. I'll always take care of you and do you know why? Because I love you. (There I said it, I hope she tells me whenever she has reached that stage in her life but I know that I will always love her. I have loved her since the very first day I took her on that blind date and I will keep loving her until the end of time. She just doesn't know it yet but I'll show her everyday with actions and words to make her fall in love with me everyday of her life.)

"I love you too baby" She touched my chest right next to my heart and said it again so I know that she also feels the same things as I do.

Wait— "Can you say it again please."

"I LOVE YOU JULIAN!!"

All I ever wanted was to be able to share these feelings with a good partner. She has exceeded my expectations. I have fallen so hard for her. She is so unique. I love her and her personality. She is my soulmate.

"I LOVE YOU TOO LUCIA"

"Thank you for making me feel loved and for choosing to move with me. I promise you won't regret it. We are going to have fun. We will have so many adventures and celebrate many things together."

Now all we have to worry about is to look for an apartment and then move in.

Chapter 10 : Bomb Sex

Lucia

We both have expressed our feelings. He said it first though. He told me he loves me and I told him I loved him back. All of this was so quick but emotions were running high. I have to confess, "I already see him as the love of my life". He makes me feel complete. I can't wait to see what our future looks like. I am sure that we will learn to live together and enjoy all of our daily adventures we are bound to have living in the same household. I was a bit upset with Julian because when we talked about looking for an apartment he told me not to worry about paying anything and I told him "Absolutely not" because I will help him pay at least some bills if he doesn't want me to pay for rent. He at least agreed with me after I told him that I would not move in if he wasn't going to allow me to help.

The next week, we started looking for affordable apartments but we weren't getting any luck. We wanted something close by, something we both know it's safe and comfortable.

My phone "pinged" announcing Julian's text message.

"Baby, do you want to come over tomorrow? My whole family is going out of town, we are going to have the whole house to ourselves."

"Yeah, I'll be around noon, If that's okay? I have errands to run before I can go to your house."

"That sounds great actually because it gives me time to clean and shower. See you tomorrow baby, I love you."

"I love you too."

In the morning, I went to do all of my errands spending almost the whole morning out. I came back home to shower and change. I left the house around 12:30 pm to head to Julian's place. When I arrived, he was already waiting for me outside his house with open arms. He looked so sexy there just standing, you can tell he just showered because his hair was still damped. Rolling down my window I said, "Hey you mister! Can I get your number? You are so handsome!"

He giggled, "Heyyy, I don't think my girlfriend would appreciate you trying to get my number" I smirked, rolling my windows up again so I can turn the car off. I got out and the first thing I did was jump his bones. He carried me adjusting my leg to be around his waist. The passionate kiss led to him getting a boner. Whispering in my ear, "Baby, I need to put you down before the neighbors see some action that is most likely going to happen if I don't let you go."

When he took me inside the house, we both had desperation in our eyes. He backed me up until my back was touching the wall. Julian kissed me on my neck then my lips, when he took a step back to look at my face I was already heating up and turning red then he said,

"Don't be shy! baby, not with me. We don't need to do

anything you are not comfortable with. I'm happy to wait until you feel ready."

All of this made me bring back memories of when my ex didn't want to wait for me to be ready. He made me feel like I was to blame when he cheated on me. Julian has been so respectful since the first day we met. Without hesitation I told him, "Baby I am ready, I want everything with you. You make me feel safe, loved, appreciated and everything a girl is supposed to feel when they have sex the first time with a new partner. I might not be a virgin anymore but you will erase all the other bad memories with good ones."

As if I just declared my love or something he caressed my cheeks.

"Are you sure baby, I want you to be completely sure before we move forward." I nodded before I took his lips on mine.

He kissed me back, the kiss took my breath away. He pushed his tongue in and I followed by giving him mine. I walked towards his room tugging him along. Julian played with the hem of my shirt while savoring my lips. Pushed his fingers inside of my shirt touching the end of my bra. His fingers continued to slip inside until I felt the callosity of the tip of his finger play with my nipple. He murmured to my ear, "It's this okay?" I bobbed my head without a word. "You gotta use your words baby, I can stop if you want"

"No please, please—"

"Please what baby"

"Don't stop, I want you" signaling him to take me to bed.

In bed, we both took each other's shirts and oh my God what a sight! His chest, his stomach was toned as if he takes his time going to the gym everyday. At the look of his fitted body, I became self conscious of my own body like I always have. This would be the first time that he was going to see me naked and It was making me pull all my worse thoughts. Terrified that he would judge me for having stretch marks from gaining weight in high school. Terrified that he was going to not like my love handles. Terrified that he would see my boobs that are slightly different in size.

"Baby, you don't have to hide your body. Your body is so hot. I've been wanting to touch you this intimately since I saw you on our first date. Those boobs are so fuckable. This ass is mine! It has a lot of meat for me to grab." making me feel a little better of my body, I took off my bra letting them free. His brown eyes were glowing. He did not want to wait any longer so he laid me down in bed with his hands on the hem of my underwear and pants, he peeled off both leaving me completely bare. Thank God that I waxed the day before. Brown eyes still glowing with lust, he dropped to his knees at the edge of the bed. I lifted myself to look at him to see what he was doing when I felt his hands on my thighs. He pulled me down so my bare ass was almost hanging out of bed.

"Oh you don't have to do that baby." blurting the words out of my mouth before he could do anything else more.

"Trust me, I want to! I want to eat this pussy. I want to taste all of you before I put my dick inside you."

I don't know who this person is—giggling "This side of you is sexy, your dirty talk is hot, making me more in heat."

"Oh you like when I talk dirty, you naughty girl? You are about to cum so hard with my tongue and my cock inside you baby."

He stopped talking and got to work, He coated his fingers with my arousal as he worked them pushing them inside. Curling his fingers to hit the exact spot where I know it takes me to heaven. My orgasm was nearing when he pushed another finger in. It was too intense and sensitive but I didn't want him to stop. He took one look at me and grinned so hard knowing I just came on his fingers and tongue. Pulling his fingers out he gets himself undressed from the waist down. He grabs his pants off the floor to take out his wallet from the back pocket. Took me a second to acknowledge what he was doing, he was taking out a condom from his wallet. Tearing the packet up with his teeth, his hand cupped his erection stroking it before putting the condom in. He took a step forward getting on top of me to part my legs wide. He put his cock at the entrance of my sex, caressing the sides before pushing inside me. I was not going to last, It was too much.

He began to thrust so hard making me have a total of 3 orgasm in minutes.

"Wow" "I can't believe what I've been missing, this is by far the best sex I've ever had baby" It was so hard to breathe, my heart was hyperventilating, it felt as if I was going to have a heart attack.

"We just had bomb sex baby." Julian kissed my forehead before throwing himself to the other side of the bed to rest. We both fell asleep for a little bit then he got up to clean me up and himself. After getting cleaned up, both of our stomachs growled. We both turned to each other to giggle. Julian ordered my favorite food "Italian" and when it got to his house, we devoured it so fast that it left us wanting more. Once we went back to bed to rest, we could not keep our eyes off each other. I was extremely happy and feeling so complete. No amount of suffering that I endured in the past could take away this moment. This man is definitely for me, and he is mine!

Weeks after we had sex, we continued to look for apartments

we couldn't keep having sex at our parent's place. We wanted to move in together now more than ever. After great sex, there was no way we could pass the opportunity of not being intimate, let alone wait longer to have sex again. It was a bit difficult to plan accordingly because there was no privacy in our homes. Four months have passed and we finally put an offer to see an apartment which ended up being perfect for both of us. We moved in at the beginning of August to a one bedroom apartment in a new city. We couldn't be happier with this step into our journey of being the best version of ourselves. Hand in hand together in love ready to face anything that comes our way.

Julian

It's been a month since we moved into this apartment that is about 25 minutes away from our job. Can't even begin to explain how we feel every time we get home from a day of work to see each other. She waits for me to get home, has dinner served and then at night we have lots of cuddles. She doesn't have to worry about anything, she does not need to pay any bills because that's what I'm here for. I work a 10-12 hour shift and work my ass off for her to have everything but my little lady is so independent that she still wants to work to help me out so I worked out a deal with her to use her money to surprise me with my favorite snacks or other things she wants to get me or something that I might need. She also does not need to have dinner served or anything but I love when she does because she shows me she cares about me. Living with her has made me learn a few more things about her. Her love language is an act of service so I do help out at home to show my appreciation for her as well. My love language is physical touch, she loves to be touchy and I appreciate that a lot. I love when she hugs me and my favorite is when she puts her fingers through my hair to rub that back of my neck. It just soothes me, making me melt into her anytime she does that. She is the greatest thing that has happened to me. I'm thankful everyday to be able to be in her space and surround myself with her. I'm so in love. We haven't had any disagreement at the moment, I am hoping i don't fuck it up because I can be a mess sometimes. I tend to leave my shit everywhere, I have a difficult time picking after myself at times. Lucky me, she has always been super understanding about my job with the strict schedule we are on. Even though I work hard, she is my priority and I show her this every single day.

Lucia

Living with Julian has been the absolute best. Except that his work keeps him for lots of hours on end and when he gets home he is super tired. I am very understanding about it since he is the one paying for everything plus he loves his job. He has never failed me even if he is tired from work, he still gives me great sex and out of this world orgasms. It's been a couple of months now of living together, not only have we become closer but we are more in love than ever. We have learned so much from each other and also ourselves. When he is at work, I am also at work or school. The finishing stages of my major are around the corner for me and soon I will be graduating. I've been thinking of looking for a different job that leads me to having more experience in the career that I'm studying in school.

Julian and I were talking about babies the other day. I've never really thought about kids before. I never really wanted them when I was younger but now that I am with Julian, I want to have all of his babies. I already know that he would look good as a daddy. He is so attentive, caring and responsible. I know he would be the greatest father for our future children. After our talk about babies we didn't discuss it again. We kept our daily routine for months until I graduated from school after 3 months of studying hard and completing all of the projects the professors assigned. I also started a new job which I'm proud of, this is giving me more access to a flexible schedule.

Chapter 11 : Surprise Surprise!

Lucia

Julian's birthday is around the corner. My plan was to celebrate it at a nice restaurant, a birthday cake and play board games all night but he had other plans in mind. Julian decided to surprise me instead. When I walked into our little apartment there were rose petals everywhere on the floor leading towards the living room. Our dinner table had fake candles lighting up the house spelling out "Marry me". I was speechless, I couldn't contain my happiness. I turned around to find him behind me with a bouquet of roses. I figure he had just finished showering because he smelled so good, his hair was still damp. I didn't even notice at first that he had a bouquet of roses in his hands.

"Lucia, I know this may be a bit rushed and soon since we've been together for 8 months, but I know that I want to spend the rest of my life with you. Will you make me the happiest man in the world and marry me?" I couldn't stop tearing with a shaky hand. I grabbed onto him and said "YES!" He opened the small box to reveal the most beautiful ring which he then proceeded to put on the ring on my ring finger. Our families were really happy for us when we finally revealed our news about the proposal. We both decided to plan for the wedding to be in a year or two, to give us time to get my dress, his tuxedo, to make sure we reserved the venue, the food and any other ideas we had. The month after Julian proposed I found out that I was pregnant. When Julian and I had talked about kids, we had initially said that we wanted to wait because he wanted to spend as much time alone being able to travel without having to worry about kids. Julian and I had begun to have sex without a condom 6 months into the relationship since I had told him that I was on birth control. The month before the proposal I had forgotten to take my pills for 2 days. This is the reason, I'm guessing how I got pregnant. I was shaking nervously for the minutes to pass by, I had bought 3 pregnancy tests to confirm my suspicions. Julian was at work and I was all alone. My timer went off letting me know it was time to check the tests. My widened eyes couldn't believe it, there it was the 2 pink lines and the word pregnant of one of the tests. With tears in my eyes I decided to get in my car and drive to the closest retail store to get something to surprise Julian with the news. I ended up buying a small box to put a baby pacifier, a baby Pajama and the 3 pregnancy tests with a card. Julian came home from work late, I had his dinner ready for him but something caught his eye in the room since the door was opened. Instead of heading to the kitchen table he went to the room where the first thing he saw was the wrapped up box. He turned to me,

"Baby, what's this?"

"It's a gift for you."

"But why baby, what's the special occasion?"

"Just open it please."

He pulled the string from the box to open it and went still. It took him a couple of minutes until he took his eyes off the box to meet mine.

"Are you sure baby?"

"Yes baby, I am! I took all 3 pregnancy tests this morning and they were all positive. I still need to get an appointment with a doctor to fully confirm how many weeks I am currently."

No more words came from him, thinking I scared him or maybe he is not ready but all he did was pull me to him to hug me and then I felt his tears on my cheek. Pulling away to take a look at him, he had the biggest smile telling me that he was excited for this new addition and journey we are about to go through together. The first trimester went by quickly with no symptoms. Thankfully because I heard otherwise from different people with different experiences. The second trimester came by with some symptoms like hot flashes and cravings. Our doctor told us we are having a boy making us the first from our family to have a boy first. The Third Trimester was the slowest. We made our birth plan and had our baby shower where all of our family and friends showed up to welcome our baby boy with so many gifts. Julian was in charge of the name for our son, He decided to name him Ezra.

Around 36 weeks, we had to face some complications, in one of those weekly doctor appointments our doctor became concerned with the baby's heart rate. Ezra's heart rate was low making it dangerous for him to be in the womb. The doctor told us to go to the emergency room to be induced. At the emergency room I was given medication for my body to start the contractions. The medication started to do its job by the second day in the middle of the night where I kept going to the bathroom to throw up. I wasn't able to get any rest, my body was drained. After hours of not being able to dilate, they had me walk around the inside of the hospital. Once back in the hospital bed I was given a peanut ball to be put in between my legs to help with dilation but that didn't help a lot. I don't know how long after that, but I slept so little then the nurse came in to check on me and said that I was still not dilating so they opted for the next option which was to insert a saline balloon inside my vagina and start pumping it with saline fluid every hour until I was fully at 10 cm. Once I was fully dilated, I pushed about 5 times, Ezra announced himself with his cry, he was born that evening very healthy. Julian and I were overjoyed to have our baby in our arms. I was released from the hospital 2 days later, making us a family of 3. Many sleepless nights during the newborn stage.

Six months later my mom gifted me my wedding dress after trying so many until I found the "one" perfect dress. We signed the contract with the venue and the catering place. I was ecstatic that we were only months away from being married. I was most excited to be able to have Ezra there with us even though he is still a baby and won't remember it.

Julian

We have our beautiful Ezra with us, we are 5 months away from getting married. To be completely honest, I never thought or pictured myself having kids or getting married. Life teaches you a thing or two when you grow and fall in love. Lucia has been my rock, she completes me, She is so resilient, strong and the one that holds us together. I loved seeing her pregnant knowing my baby was inside her womb. She has always been beautiful but with pregnancy she glowed anywhere she went. I planned our honeymoon making it a surprise for Lucia. She has been busy planning the wedding with her sister. I bought our marriage band rings and it will go beautifully with the engagement ring I proposed with. After having Ezra, Lucia decided not to go back to work for a while because she wanted to be able to stay home with him as much as possible, which meant I had to work extra hard to get more income. I didn't mind though, I love being a hard worker and now I get to do it for her, for Ezra, for my little family that I created with Lucia. She is going to go wild when she figures out that I am taking her to Hawaii for our honeymoon. Our little Ezra will stay with Lucia's mom in the meantime. I can't wait to get there and get started on baby number 2 with my lady. Can't wait to call her "My wife". It's getting closer, she will be my wife "Mine".

Lucia

On the day of our wedding, we celebrated with our friends and family. It was the most spectacular day because it was the day that we sealed our names together on a piece of paper. We became one. Now I get to call Julian "My husband" It has a nice ring to it. I better start practicing now,

"Husband"

Julian chuckles because he loves hearing me call him that.

"Baby, I have a surprise for you."

"Yeah? What is it?"

"Let's get home, we will put Ezra to sleep then I can show you after but you will need to pack your bags tonight because tomorrow we have to leave Ezra with your mom so we can go to our honeymoon"

My mother had offered to stay with Ezra so we could have our honeymoon like every couple should. When we got home Julian gave me the tickets revealing our destination for our honeymoon.

"I've never been to Hawaii baby, thank you. We are going to have so much fun."

When we got to the destination, Julian wanted to start right away in baby making and I wasn't opposed to it because I want my little Ezra to have a sibling. After having Ezra, I had a bit of complications with my cycle, my periods became irregular. It became hard to plan accordingly but we both said we didn't need to worry about it. It will happen eventually and when it does we can go from there as to planning. We had 4 amazing days in Hawaii. When I came back from our honeymoon trip everything was going so well until it wasn't. Julian and I were okay, not the greatest but we started fighting here and there. I think it was the pressure of him working too many hours and pushing himself to the point that he was overworking himself. We needed to find a way to make this work because we said to each other that we will face any obstacle together.

Julian

Back from our honeymoon everything felt great but once I came back to work I started working long hours, six days a week. I started feeling it in my body, the tiredness, the lack of sleep, the joint pains. I didn't want to tell Lucia about it but we needed the extra money now that we had to buy things for Ezra. I also started spending money on unnecessary things here and there to support my expensive hobbies. I just didn't tell Lucia what I was spending the money on, she clearly found it odd that I was working extra hours and I was also getting packages after packages delivered at home. Little arguments arose which was not my intention at all, I knew I had to share my secret hobby. She understood me after I told her everything. I should've told her my plan from the beginning. The arguments stopped, she even got to learn more about my hobby. Everything went well in the end until I had an accident. In a blink of an eye, I got injured at work that required me to be taken to the hospital immediately. Something that pissed me off was that no one called my wife but I also didn't want anyone to tell her the severity of my injuries. She was with Ezra, I didn't want her to faint or worry about this situation. At the hospital the doctors had given me my diagnosis. That's when I decided to call Lucia.

"Baby, I need you to sit down and listen to me okay." I said it calmly so she doesn't get scared even though I knew she would be either way.

"Baby, you are scaring me, what happened?"

"I'm at the hospital, I had an accident at work. The doctors just told me that they are going to prepare me to go into surgery soon. I need you to come to me." All I could hear was Lucia's sobbing in the background.

Chapter 12 : The Accident

Lucia

That call was the most devastating call I've ever gotten in my life. It got me so worried that I was pale as a ghost, I couldn't think straight. After my husband called to tell me that he got into an accident at work and that he was at the hospital about to go into surgery my heart shattered. I couldn't contain my cry. I went to my mom's to leave Ezra with her while I drove to the hospital to pick him up. Confused as to why they were letting him go if he was about to have surgery. I wanted to be by his side. I kept talking to myself on the drive to the hospital "How bad was the accident that happened at work? It must have been a terrible one for him to have surgery right away."

When I got to the hospital I was drained. I couldn't think straight but I needed to be okay for Julian. I don't want to think of any of the possibilities that might happen with a surgery like this. I needed to stop thinking of the worst case scenarios and think positive.

"Hello, I'm here because my husband was brought into the emergency room."

The nice lady in the front could tell that I had been crying, my eyes were swollen.

"I will let the doctor know that you are here okay, take a seat in the waiting area."

The doctor came out and guided me to the room where Julian was resting from surgery. When I got inside the room the main surgeon explained the severity of his accident. He explained that Julian had fallen from a high place while cleaning the section he was in charge of. When he came up to stand up he couldn't stand on his leg he had shattered his foot into tiny pieces. The doctor said that it was a difficult surgery, they basically said he could've had his foot amputated but thankfully they were able to put a metal plate to hold the bone together. It's been a hectic day for all of us, I am sure Julian is terrified about everything that comes next for him, his foot, his job. Julian barely opened his eyes, he was still drowsy from the medication.

"Hi baby, how are you feeling" I know it's a stupid question given that he is in the emergency room with this kind of injury but I still wanted to know how he was feeling.

"I'm feeling okay baby, don't worry. What did the doctors say? When can we leave?"

I told him everything they said, Julian rubbed the bridge of his nose like he wanted to contain his teary eyes. He huffed so loud that I knew he was having a hard time with everything that was said to him. We waited for them to discharge him. We picked up Ezra and headed home. After getting home it was difficult getting him inside the apartment. We both knew it would be a long journey for us to get through this. Julian was told he needed to rest for six months, he couldn't put any pressure on his foot while it healed. In those six months he became stressed, irritated about everything, maybe even depressed and I understood because he had to rely on everyone else to do things for him. Not working also made him very grumpy since he loves what he does at work.

Julian

I'm not feeling optimistic. I want to go back in time to the exact moment of my injury to prevent it from happening. I am miserable here at home not doing anything and I am going crazy because I can't do anything for myself. I have to have my beautiful wife deal with me and Ezra. I don't want to be a burden to her. It makes me grumpy all the time not being able to do anything on my own.

"FUCK!— PIECE OF SHIT—(shattering sound)."

Lucia came out of the room to check on me since I had thrown my crutches to the floor.

"Are you okay, need any help?"

"NO, I don't need any fucking help Lucia."

"Okay, sorry I just wanted to help." Lucia steps back into the room where I hear her sob softly. I'm a piece of shit— why the hell am I yelling at my beautiful wife when all she wants to do is help. I did need the help, I was just being an asshole! Something else that was stressing me over was that I didn't even know if I was going to have my job back. I'm supposed to be the main provider for my family. I became depressed, I kept to myself and slept a lot to hide my pain. Lucia kept wanting to help me with everything but anything she did for me was annoying me, I wanted to be able to do it on my own. She noticed my emotions. Lucia said we needed to talk, she did the talking mostly, I just listened. She reminded me that there is a reason we chose each other as partners, as spouses, and that she was going to keep our family from going down. She told me she will keep doing things for me until I get better.

"Our ups and downs are not just for one person to deal with, it's for both of us to face together."

After the heartfelt talk she had with me, I knew I had to change my ways. It became easier when I was told that my foot was healing perfectly. I was sent in to do physical therapy to strengthen my foot. I worked hard to make my foot stronger. It was still a long journey because it hurt like a bitch to put pressure. After months of physical therapy my foot became stronger then I was given a boot to continue putting pressure on it. It's been 5 months since my injury. I've been to multiple doctors to tell me what's wrong with my swelling but no one can tell me anything. I started to notice that even with physical therapy that my foot was still swelling from time to time when I would over do it in walking or putting my weight on it. My surgeon said that I might need another surgery down the line but I'm scared to go through that again. It's a scary place, I never want to feel like that in my life again. It wasn't easy for me, for Lucia and for Ezra. I hate not being able to run after my kid for hours without my foot hurting or swelling up.

Lucia

It's been six months since Julian's injury. He goes back to work next week. I am hoping they take it easy on him even though Julian doesn't want to show it off. I can see he struggles from time to time and it makes me sad that he doesn't want to share that with me. I understand he is trying to protect me from hurting but I want him to tell me what he feels so maybe we can have a second opinion to get to a solution. We decided to put our plans of having our second baby on standby, we wanted to focus on Julian getting better. Ezra is growing so fast, he is running wild. He looks so much like Julian.

"Ezra, go tell your daddy you love him before he goes to work."

Ezra runs to Julian to pepper him with kisses.

"Luv yoo, dadda."

Julian smiles every time Ezra shows his affection to him because It's so adorable the way children talk.

"I love you too baby, I'll see you tomorrow okay. Be extra nice to mommy." (kisses his forehead and sets him down)

"I love you too honey, don't wait for me tonight. I'll be home late."

"Okay baby, drive safe and be careful at work with your injured foot okay."

Kissing me passionately before smacking my ass and heading to the door to leave. After Julian got back to work, weeks went by. He adjusted himself to work long hours and still managed to get back home without complaining. Julian is my superhero, he has endured so much. We are the most important people in his life no matter what he is going through he will always support his family until the end.

Chapter 13 : Infertility

Lucia

We officially started trying for baby number 2, It's been a year since Julian's Injury. Julian felt more enthusiastic to have another baby, he wanted Ezra to have a sibling. I stopped taking birth control hoping that I would get pregnant the same way as I did with Ezra. We started to worry that we were not succeeding. With Ezra it took me a month after stopping birth control to get pregnant, with the second baby it's not happening. A month, then two, then three until month six of trying and nothing was happening. We were losing our faith. I searched all over the internet for something to give me motivation but nothing was making me feel better. I started going to the doctor, took a bunch of exams, blood work, and ultrasounds.

The only answer they came up with was that I was going through a hormonal imbalance. They gave me information on how to balance it but it can take time. It's been a year that we've been trying to get pregnant and it still hasn't happened even with all the instructions from the doctor. I made an appointment with a fertility physician to see if there were other underlying issues. Doing this because before I was having irregular cycles which made it a lot more difficult to track ovulation. They did more blood work, everything was normal again. I still did not have a solution so I pressed my fertility physician to dig deeper. The fertility consultation was to give us information on how the treatments were planned for me. I was given medication to ovulate, then an injection just in case I didn't. I got a total of 2-3 ultrasounds to check if any follicles were growing. I did more blood work that came back normal again. We did everything they required from us. We didn't want to give up but even with the treatments being expensive and tiring we still tried. We did a couple of sessions with no luck. We spent thousands of dollars trying to have successful tries but It was not successful every time.

"Baby, open the door." (knocking sound)

"Please, leave me, I need alone time at the moment." sobbing

"Lucia, we can face this together, you don't need to cry all by yourself. Please let me in."

I would secretly cry when I was alone for hours and hours until I had no more tears left to shed. I was struggling with the reality of the issue. I wasn't able to get pregnant even with the help of a specialist. Julian wanted to keep doing the treatments but I don't want it to fail again, it's too painful. It stresses me out. I don't know if I am strong enough to get bad news again because every time I take a pregnancy test, it ends up being negative. It's shattering my heart in pieces. After I finally convinced Julian about stopping all treatment of the insemination procedure I had a little bit of relief about everything. My mental health and my sanity was thanking me. It pained me like hell having to come to that decision because that just meant that my hopes of having another baby were less of a reality. I didn't have a lot of faith left. Things happen for a reason, I will continue to go through life thanking God for my beautiful Ezra at least since I can't have another one.

Julian

It makes me incredibly sad to see my wife cry. It breaks my heart because I hate seeing her this way. When she went in to see the doctors and specialist about our problem with not getting pregnant, I thought it would be a better solution but the results were draining us. I know she is trying to keep this confidence and she thinks that I don't see it but I know her so well, I know she is breaking on the inside. I find her in every inch of this apartment with her shedding tears. She thinks I don't notice it, well I see everything. I wish I could take her pain away. We have to stay positive and have faith that we will win our battles. Spending a couple thousand trying with multiple sessions but we have not been victorious. Lucia pulled me to the side and told me she did not want to continue the treatment because it was too much for her. She practically begged me to stop that her mental health was first and we just needed to come to terms that we will only have Ezra.

"What's not meant to be it's not meant to be" Lucia said when she had pulled me to the side of our last appointment. It broke me but if she did not want to continue I will be with her every step of the way.

"Baby, one day we will have our little miracle, I swear to you."

"Julian, please don't promise me something that might not

come true."

"Lucia, think positive please, we have to keep manifesting it okay."

Lucia 3 years later

"Julian, what are you doing?" I yelped

"Baby, we have about 2 hours until we pick up Ezra from school. I'm about to make you mine."

"I am yours! Baby."

"I know you're mine honey, but I just want to make you feel good."

Julian pulled me into the room, tossing me in the bed. He undressed me and got to work.

We both picked up Ezra from school. I can't believe my child, my little baby has grown so much. He is a smart kid. I am not going to lie but I do get sad from time to time when Ezra asks when he is going to have a little brother or sister but it just hasn't happened for us. I have come to terms already and I am not stressing over it.

"Baby, are you okay? You look pale." running off to the bathroom to throw up

"I think I ate something that upset my stomach." I just had food from a fast food place and It was greasy, I think that's what made me sick. After a week I was still throwing up and losing weight which made me worry that it might be something other than the stomach flu. I arranged for an appointment the next day to get blood work done. My doctor called me to give me the results the day after I got my blood work done,

"Good morning, May I speak with Mrs. Vega?"

"Yes, this is her." I said.

"Mrs. Vega, I am calling to talk to you about your test results. I know you came in yesterday to do blood work to verify if anything was going on since you were feeling sick, is that correct?" she said.

"Yes that's right, were my results normal?"

"All of your test results came back normal Mrs. Vega, but we did find one of the tests that was elevated." she said.

"It's this the reason why I've been feeling sick?"

"Yes, it's part of the reason but you don't have to worry, Mrs. Vega. Your HCG test came back positive "You're Pregnant Mrs. Vega congratulations." I was dumbstruck, I had lost my voice, there was no communication after this, I ended the call. I didn't mean to be rude but I just needed to come to terms with this new revelation.

Chapter 14: Our Happy Ending

Lucia

I forgot how to speak, all these years of trying, money being used to get just a little bit of hope and nothing happened until now. Getting the news of me being pregnant, It's surreal, I didn't even know how I was going to bring the news to Julian. He wasn't even home at the moment because he was with Ezra at the park. I decided to quickly leave the house and head over to the store to get a couple of things to surprise him. The best news I could possibly give him. Julian got home about thirty minutes later while I was setting everything up. I had bought baby clothes, a pacifier and then I also bought a pregnancy test to take. After I took the test I included everything in the box and set it up on the coffee table for him to open. It was almost the same box I surprised him with our first baby.

"Babe, what did you get me? What is this gift box on our table?" I was shaking and tearing uncontrollably, I couldn't contain my happiness knowing that I'm carrying our second baby. That I get to do it all over again with the person I love dearly.

"Open it baby, but close your eyes first and then open them." Pulling the string of the box Julian opened the box.

"Can I open my eyes now."

"Yeah, you can open them."

Julian took a good look at the inside of the box, then his brown eyes got all teary and shifted his gaze at my eyes. My eyes could tell him everything my voice couldn't.

"Are you sure—?" swallowing the gulp that had caught up between his throat because he was unsure of what was happening. My heart skipped a beat just looking at my husband in disbelief since we were waiting for this to happen many years ago. We already had come to terms that we would not be getting pregnant but life works in mysterious ways sometimes.

"Yes, babe the doctor just called to tell me my tests came back normal but she also confirmed that I'm pregnant" His jaw-dropped, no words came out but a grin from cheek to cheek beamed on his face. Hugs, kisses and tears of joy were the only thing in this room.

"I love you."

"I love you more honey."

Months flew by showing my swollen belly. We are thankful and grateful for this new addition. Ezra can't wait to finally be an older brother. Julian is indulging every moment he can and I am too since this will be our last baby. Telling our families will be fun. Now we just need to wait to learn the gender of our baby. Ezra wants a baby brother, I want a boy as well but then there's Julian who wants a baby girl.

Julian

When Lucia told me she was pregnant, I sobbed. We finally did it! We tried everything to make this happen after all the failed attempts. Now here we are going to experience this all over again. Our family is delighted with the news. We are soon to be a family of 4. I can't wait to see Ezra being a big brother. We are cherishing this moment as a family. My wife looks more than beautiful with her round belly. I told Lucia I wanted to have a baby girl this time, but as long as the baby is healthy it won't matter if it's a girl or a boy. Lucia wants a boy because she thinks that if it's a girl that she will lose the attention I give her and give it to the baby. She wants to be the only girl. I reminded her that she will always be my queen and if we have a baby girl then she will be the princess. To me it's important to show my wife that she is the woman of my dreams, she has gone through tough shit but she is still standing tall with her chin high. That woman is everything. I don't know what I would do without her. Can't wait to see what our future holds for us as a family of 4.

Lucia

The second and third trimester flew by at full throttle, I didn't even feel as if I was pregnant for long. The next thing I know is that we were in the hospital ready for me to give birth. There were a total of 3 pushes then our little man was welcomed into this world. "Oh yeah we found out we were having a baby boy" I told Julian that he only makes boys, his response to that was just giggles after giggles. Our baby boy came to us healthy, big and strong. We named him Levi, he is the most adorable baby. Not just because he is my baby but because everyone who has seen him says the same. He looks a lot like me, which is the opposite of Ezra, who looks like Julian. Levi has dark curls, golden brown skin tone. His eyes and nose are similar to mine, where Ezra has straight black hair, olive skin and has similar features to Julian. It's been exactly a month since I've given birth to our second precious baby boy Levi. He has been the highlight of this family. Knowing that people go through infertility saddens me. I never knew we needed Levi until I had him in my arms, I had already come to terms with just having one child but we definitely needed Levi. It's adorable seeing Ezra being the best big brother. Julian is the best husband and father I could have chosen. When he is holding Levi in his arms and Ezra in the other, every obstacle or hassle that I went through makes it worth the result. As for me I am very blessed I got to experience being a mom a second time. A lot of women suffer from infertility. A lot of them don't know the causes and they try for months, years with no success. My advice to any woman is to never give up hope.

Yes, you can take a break but don't lose your faith, keep trying. There is no success without risk. All we want from now on is to enjoy life, give it our best at being parents, we want to make sure we teach our kids to be the best versions of themselves and for them to always have self love, self respect, kindness, morals, be responsible, to have fun and most importantly to always be their true self. The future has great things for us, I just know it! I do have lots of questions though.

What will my boys do when they grow up? Will I still be here when they have their own family? Will Julian and I travel the world falling more madly in love? These thoughts secretly flooded my mind. We just have to live day by day. Only time will tell but until then we will continue to be the best version of ourselves for each other, for our kids and for our family.

Epilogue

Ezra 27 years old

I can't believe that in a few more months I'll be 28 years old. It's been a long journey. I'll be forever grateful to be lucky enough to have the best parents in the world, they have shown all of their love to us as any parents should. We know mom never had a father figure in her life so she never experienced a fatherly love like I did from my dad. Mom chose the right person to have kids with, my dad not only made a promise to love her but to always take care of her. Mom has made it to her fifties. She is still my dad's greatest love. She is no longer working, she decided to become a romance book author. She writes all about romance, she always says she is a hopeless romantic. Writing is everything to her. She gets to imagine, tell a story, romanticize and relate to other readers and writers. My dad is in his fifties too, he is working part time still but is also doing what he loves on the side by collecting gaming cards. Lately mom and dad have been traveling to different destinations while Levi and I hang out and bond over games. They have traveled to many places falling in love all over again but they always go back to their favorite place where they reminisce about all of the memories they have about their honeymoon in Hawaii. My mom always wondered what I would be doing when I grow up, well she doesn't have to question it anymore. I am working for a big gaming company doing what I love! I have my own little apartment with the help of my dad. I met a girl that I fell in love with. My girlfriend and I both met also in a non-traditional way just like my parents. Mom and dad have loved each other for more than 30 years, I want to have a love like theirs with my girlfriend. I've been thinking for a while of proposing to my girlfriend and I am super ecstatic that my parents love her and are supportive of her.

I still visit my parents often since they want me to stay with Levi when they go on trips. Levi is still in school and loves to have me around because we both have fun playing video games. We used to fight all the time when I was younger but now that I'm all grown we get to talk, go out, confide in each other and have fun. He looks up to me as a role model, he trusts me to speak his mind and I'm glad he is able to see me as that person. Mom and dad think that they won't be here past 70 "I know, right? My parents are silly to say this." Dad still deals with a lot of pain from his foot injury and mom has a lot of health issues. It's sad, I wish I could always have my parents but It's the cycle of life and I know once the time comes, they will be taking care of me and my brother Levi from anywhere they are. We try to spend most of our time together. Sundays are for fun nights with my parents and all of our family. We get together to play games, eat food, sing karaoke, connect and bond with each other. To me the most important thing is to cherish every moment I have with them. They have given me the best 27 years of my life and I am extremely grateful to have them as parents.

I love you mom and dad!

The End..

About the Author

V. Elias is a romance book author. She is a mom, a wife and cat lover. She is 32 years old. Her love for books began when she started reviewing books for fun on social media. In high school her favorite subject was English/Literature and psychology. She always wanted to write, act and sing. V. Elias has a background in social and behavioral science, Criminal Justice and Psychology. She wants to catch a reader's mind by sharing unique love stories. The plan for her next books are to go into a dark theme to surprise the readers with an amazing dark romance plot. Please continue to share your ideas, your voice and your skills with the world. Hard work is always acknowledged.

You can connect with me on:

- https://www.instagram.com/v.eliasauthor
- https://www.tiktok.com/@v.eliasauthor

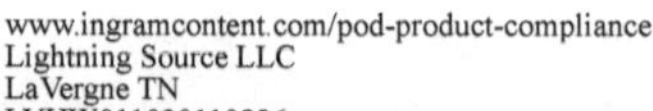

www.ingramcontent.com/pod-product-compliance
Lightning Source LLC
LaVergne TN
LVHW011030110826
845149LV00015B/3361

9798994733110